Alf Prøysen

Mʀs PEPPERPOT STORIES

Mrs Pepperpot Stories

Things are pretty difficult for Mrs Pepperpot – she is never sure if she is going to be her normal size, or tiny like a pepperpot. How can she go and see her friends, get the supper cooked, and stop the cat from thinking she is a mouse? And what will be her fate when she gets stuck in a drawer of macaroni at the grocers?

Mrs Pepperpot's hilarious adventures as she copes with these difficulties will have you in stitches.

Alf Prøysen was born in Norway, and has written stories (including other *Mrs Pepperpot* stories) and poems for children, a weekly newspaper column and a series of programmes for radio.

Alf Prøysen

LITTLE OLD Mrs PEPPERPOT

Illustrated by Björn Berg

RED FOX

A Red Fox Book

Published by Random House Children's Books
20 Vauxhall Bridge Road, London SW1V 2SA

A division of Random House UK Ltd
London Melbourne Sydney Auckland
Johannesburg and agencies throughout the world

Little Old Mrs Pepperpot
First published by Hutchinson Junior Books 1959
Beaver edition 1984, Reprinted 1985 (twice), 1987, 1989 and 1990
Copyright © text Alf Prøyson 1959
Copyright © English translation Hutchinson 1959

Mrs Pepperpot Again
First published by Hutchinson Children's Books 1960
Beaver edition 1985, Reprinted 1986 (twice), and 1988
Red Fox edition 1991
Copyright © Alf Prøyson 1960
English translation © Century Hutchinson 1960

Mrs Pepperpot's Outing
First published by Hutchinson Children's Books 1971
Beaver edition 1988, Reprinted 1988 and 1989 (twice)
Copyright © text Alf Prøysen 1969
English translation © Hutchinson Children's Books 1971

First published in this edition by Red Fox 1992
17 19 20 18 16

Printed and bound in Great Britain by
The Guernsey Press Co. Ltd, Guernsey, Channel Islands

RANDOM HOUSE UK Ltd Reg No 954009

ISBN 0 09 914121 3

Contents

Little old Mrs. Pepperpot

THERE was once an old woman who went to bed at night as old women usually do, and in the morning she woke up as old women usually do. But on this particular morning she found herself shrunk to the size of a pepperpot, and old women don't usually do that. The odd thing was, her name really was Mrs. Pepperpot.

'Well, as I'm now the size of a pepperpot, I shall have to make the best of it,' she said to herself, for she had no one else to talk to; her husband was out in the fields and all her children were grown up and gone away.

Now she happened to have a great deal to do that day. First of all she had to clean the house, then there was all the washing which was lying in soak and waiting to be done, and lastly she had to make pancakes for supper.

'I must get out of bed somehow,' she thought, and, taking hold of a corner of the eiderdown, she started rolling herself up in it. She rolled and rolled until the eiderdown was like a huge sausage, which fell softly on the floor. Mrs. Pepperpot crawled out and she hadn't hurt herself a bit.

The first job was to clean the house, but that was quite easy; she just sat down in front of a mouse-hole and squeaked till the mouse came out.

'Clean the house from top to bottom,' she said, 'or I'll tell the cat about you.' So the mouse cleaned the house from top to bottom.

Mrs. Pepperpot called the cat: 'Puss! Puss! Lick out all the plates and dishes or I'll tell the dog about you.' And the cat licked all the plates and dishes clean.

Then the old woman called the dog. 'Listen, dog; you make the bed and open the window and I'll give you a bone as a reward.' So the dog did as he was told, and when he had finished he sat down on the front door-step and waved his tail so hard he made the step shine like a mirror.

'You'll have to get the bone yourself,' said Mrs. Pepperpot, 'I haven't time to wait on people.' She pointed to the window-sill where a large bone lay.

After this she wanted to start her washing. She had put it to soak in the brook, but the brook was almost dry. So she sat down and started muttering in a discontented sort of way:

'I have lived a long time, but in all my born days I never saw the brook so dry. If we don't have a shower soon, I expect everyone will die of thirst.' Over and over again she said it, all the time looking up at the sky.

At last the raincloud in the sky got so angry that it decided to drown the old woman altogether. But she crawled under a monk's-hood flower, where she stayed snug and warm while the rain poured down and rinsed her clothes clean in the brook.

Now the old woman started muttering again: 'I have lived a long time, but in all my born days I have never known such a feeble South Wind as we have had lately. I'm sure if the South Wind started blowing this minute it couldn't lift me off the ground, even though I am no bigger than a pepperpot.'

The South Wind heard this and instantly came tearing along, but Mrs. Pepperpot hid in an empty badger set, and from there she watched the South Wind blow all the clothes right up on to her clothes-line.

Again she started muttering: 'I have lived a long time, but in all my born days I have never seen the sun give so little heat in the middle of the summer. It seems to have lost all its power, that's a fact.'

When the sun heard this it turned scarlet with rage and sent down fiery rays to give the old woman sunstroke. But by this time she was safely back in her house, and was sailing about the sink in a saucer. Meanwhile the furious sun dried all the clothes on the line.

'Now for cooking the supper,' said Mrs. Pepperpot; 'my husband will be back in an hour and, by hook or by crook, thirty pancakes must be ready on the table.'

She had mixed the dough for the pancakes in a bowl the day before. Now she sat down beside the bowl and said: 'I have always been fond of you, bowl, and I've told all the neighbours that there's not a bowl like you any-where. I am sure, if you really wanted to, you could walk straight over to the cooking-stove and turn it on.'

And the bowl went straight over to the stove and turned it on.

Then Mrs. Pepperpot said: 'I'll never forget the day I bought my frying-pan. There were lots of pans in the shop, but I said: "If I can't have that pan hanging right over the shop assistant's head, I won't buy any pan at all. For that is the best pan in the whole world, and I'm sure if I were ever in trouble that pan could jump on to the stove by itself." '

And there and then the frying-pan jumped on to the stove. And when it was hot enough, the bowl tilted itself to let the dough run on to the pan.

Then the old woman said: 'I once read a fairy-tale about a pancake which could roll along the road. It was the stupidest story that ever I read. But I'm sure the pan-cake on the pan could easily turn a somersault in the air if it really wanted to.'

At this the pancake took a great leap from sheer pride and turned a somersault as Mrs. Pepperpot had said. Not only one pancake, but *all* the pancakes did this, and the bowl went on tilting and the pan went on frying until, before the hour was up, there were thirty pancakes on the dish.

Then Mr. Pepperpot came home. And, just as he opened the door, Mrs. Pepperpot turned back to her usual size. So they sat down and ate their supper.

And the old woman said nothing about having been as small as a pepperpot, because old women don't usually talk about such things.

Mrs. Pepperpot and the mechanical doll

IT WAS two days before Christmas. Mrs. Pepperpot hummed and sang as she trotted round her kitchen, she was so pleased to be finished with all her Christmas preparations. The pig had been killed, the sausages made, and now all she had to do was to brew herself a cup of coffee and sit down for a little rest.

'How lovely that Christmas is here,' she said, 'then everybody's happy—especially the children—that's the best of all; to see them happy and well.'

The old woman was almost like a child herself because of this knack she had of suddenly shrinking to the size of a pepperpot.

She was thinking about all this while she was making her coffee, and she had just poured it into the cup when there was a knock at the door.

'Come in,' she said, and in came a little girl who was oh! so pale and thin.

'Poor child! Wherever do you live—I'm sure I've never seen you before,' said Mrs. Pepperpot.

'I'm Hannah. I live in the little cottage at the edge of

the forest,' said the child, 'and I'm just going round to all the houses to ask if anybody has any old Christmas decorations left over from last year—glitter or paper-chains or glass balls or anything, you know. Have *you* got anything you don't need?'

'I expect so, Hannah,' answered Mrs. Pepperpot, and went up into the attic to fetch the cardboard box with all the decorations. She gave it to the little girl.

'How lovely! Can I really have all that?'

'You can,' said Mrs. Pepperpot, 'and you shall have something else as well. Tomorrow I will bring you a big doll.'

'I don't believe that,' said Hannah.

'Why not?'

'You haven't *got* a doll.'

'That's simple; I'll buy one,' said Mrs. Pepperpot. 'I'll bring it over tomorrow afternoon, but I must be home by six o'clock because it's Christmas Eve.'

'How wonderful if you can come tomorrow afternoon—I shall be all alone. Father and Mother both go out to work, you see, and they don't get back until the church bells have rung.'

So the little girl went home, and Mrs. Pepperpot went down to the toy-shop and bought a big doll. But when she woke up next morning there she was, once more, no bigger than a pepperpot.

'How provoking!' she said to herself. 'On this day of all days, when I have to take the doll to Hannah. Never mind! I expect I'll manage.'

After she had dressed she tried to pick up the doll, but it was much too heavy for her to lift.

'I'll have to go without it,' she thought, and opened the door to set off.

But oh dear! it had been snowing hard all night, and the little old woman soon sank deep in the snowdrifts. The cat was sitting in front of the house; when she saw something moving in the snow she thought it was a mouse and jumped on it.

'Hi, stop!' shouted Mrs. Pepperpot. 'Keep your claws to yourself! Can't you see it's just me shrunk again?'

'I beg your pardon,' said the cat, and started walking away.

'Wait a minute,' said Mrs. Pepperpot, 'to make up for your mistake you can give me a ride down to the main road.' The cat was quite willing, so she lay down and let the little old woman climb on her back. When they got to the main road the cat stopped. 'Can you hear anything?' asked Mrs. Pepperpot.

'Yes, I think it's the snow-plough,' said the cat, 'so we'll have to get out of the way, or we'll be buried in snow.'

'I don't want to get out of the way,' said Mrs. Pepper-pot, and she sat down in the middle of the road and waited till the snow-plough was right in front of her; then she jumped up and landed smack on the front tip of the plough.

There she sat, clinging on for dear life and enjoying herself hugely. 'Look at me, the little old woman, driving the snow-plough!' she laughed.

When the snow-plough had almost reached the door of Hannah's little cottage, she climbed on to the edge nearest the side of the road and, before you could say Jack Robinson, she had landed safely on the great mound of snow thrown up by the plough. From there she could walk right across Hannah's hedge and slide down the other side. She was shaking the snow off her clothes on the doorstep when Hannah came out and picked her up.

'Are you one of those mechanical dolls that you wind up?' asked Hannah.

'No,' said Mrs. Pepperpot, 'I am a woman who can wind myself up, thank you very much. Help me brush off all the snow and then let's go inside.'

'Are you perhaps the old woman who shrinks to the size of a pepperpot?'

'Of course I am, silly.'

'Where's the doll you were going to bring me?' asked Hannah when they got inside.

'I've got it at home. You'll have to go back with me and fetch it. It's too heavy for me.'

'Shouldn't you have something to eat, now that you've come to see me? Would you like a biscuit?' And the little girl held out a biscuit in the shape of a ring.

'Thank you very much,' said Mrs. Pepperpot and popped her head through the biscuit ring.

Oh, how the little girl laughed! 'I quite forgot you were so small,' she said; 'let me break it into little pieces so that you can eat it.' Then she fetched a thimble and filled it with fruit juice. 'Have a drink,' she said.

'Thank you,' said Mrs. Pepperpot.

After that they played a lot of good games; ride-a-cock-horse with Mrs. Pepperpot sitting on Hannah's knee, and hide-and-seek. But the little girl had an awful time trying to find Mrs. Pepperpot—she hid in such awkward places. When they had finished playing Hannah put on her coat and with Mrs. Pepperpot in her pocket she went off to fetch her beautiful big doll.

'Oh, thank you!' she exclaimed when she saw it. 'But do you know,' she added, 'I would really rather have *you* to play with all the time.'

'You can come and see me again if you like,' said Mrs. Pepperpot, 'I am often as small as a pepperpot, and then it's nice to have a little help around the house. And, of course, we can play games as well.'

So now the little girl often spends her time with Mrs. Pepperpot. She looks ever so much better, and they often talk about the day Mrs. Pepperpot arrived on the snow-plough, and about the doll she gave Hannah.

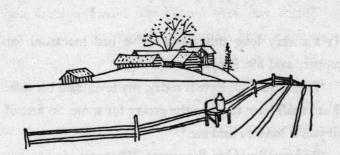

Mr. Pepperpot buys macaroni

'It's a very long time since we've had macaroni for supper,' said Mr. Pepperpot one day.

'Then you shall have it today, my love,' said his wife. 'But I shall have to go to the grocer for some. So first of all you'll have to find me.'

'Find you?' said Mr. Pepperpot. 'What sort of nonsense is that?' But when he looked round for her he couldn't see her anywhere. 'Don't be silly, wife,' he said; 'if you're hiding in the cupboard you must come out this minute. We're too big to play hide-and-seek.'

'*I'm* not too big, I'm just the right size for "hunt-the-pepperpot",' laughed Mrs. Pepperpot. 'Find me if you can!'

'I'm not going to charge round my own bedroom looking for my wife,' he said crossly.

'Now, now! I'll help you; I'll tell you when you're warm. Just now you're very cold.' For Mr. Pepperpot was peering out of the window, thinking she might have jumped out. As he searched round the room she called out 'Warm!', 'Colder!', 'Getting hotter!' until he was quite dizzy.

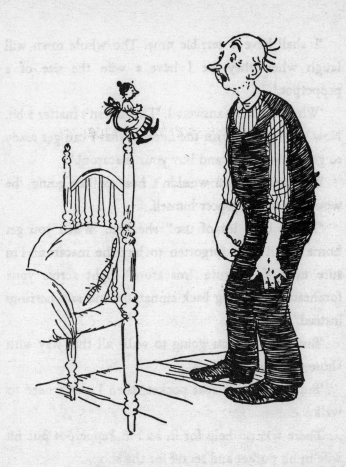

At last she shouted, 'You'll burn the top of your bald head if you don't look up!' And there she was, sitting on the bedpost, swinging her legs and laughing at him.

Her husband pulled a very long face when he saw her. 'This is a bad business—a very bad business,' he said, stroking her cheek with his little finger.

'I don't think it's a bad business,' said Mrs. Pepperpot.

'I shall have a terrible time. The whole town will laugh when they see I have a wife the size of a pepperpot.'

'Who cares?' she answered. 'That doesn't matter a bit. Now put me down on the floor so that I can get ready to go to the grocer and buy your macaroni.'

But her husband wouldn't hear of her going; he would go to the grocer himself.

'That'll be a lot of use!' she said. 'When you get home you'll have forgotten to buy the macaroni. I'm sure even if I wrote "macaroni" right across your forehead you'd bring back cinnamon and salt herrings instead.'

'But how are you going to walk all that way with those tiny legs?'

'Put me in your coat pocket; then I won't need to walk.'

There was no help for it, so Mr. Pepperpot put his wife in his pocket and set off for the shop.

Soon she started talking: "My goodness me, what a lot of strange things you have in your pocket—screws and nails, tobacco and matches—there's even a fish-hook! You'll have to take that out at once; I might get it caught in my skirt.'

'Don't talk so loud,' said her husband as he took out the fish-hook. 'We're going into the shop now.'

It was an old-fashioned village store where they sold everything from prunes to coffee cups. The grocer was particularly proud of the coffee cups and held one up for Mr. Pepperpot to see. This made his wife curious and she popped her head out of his pocket.

'You stay where you are!' whispered Mr. Pepperpot.

'I beg your pardon, did you say anything?' asked the grocer.

'No, no, I was just humming a little tune,' said Mr. Pepperpot. 'Tra-la-la!'

'What colour are the cups?' whispered his wife. And her husband sang:

> 'The cups are blue
> With gold edge too,
> But they cost too much
> So that won't do!'

After that Mrs. Pepperpot kept quiet—but not for long. When her husband pulled out his tobacco tin she couldn't resist hanging on to the lid. Neither her husband nor anyone else in the shop noticed her slipping on to the counter and hiding behind a flour-bag. From there she darted silently across to the scales, crawled under them, past a pair of kippers wrapped in newspaper, and found herself next to the coffee cups.

'Aren't they pretty!' she whispered, and took a step backwards to get a better view. Whoops! She fell right into the macaroni drawer which had been left open. She hastily covered herself up with macaroni, but the grocer heard the scratching noise and quickly banged the drawer shut. You see, it did sometimes happen that mice got in the drawers, and that's not the sort of thing you want people to know about, so the grocer pretended nothing had happened and went on serving.

There was Mrs. Pepperpot all in the dark; she could hear the grocer serving her husband now. 'That's good,' she thought. 'When he orders macaroni I'll get my chance to slip into the bag with it.'

But it was just as she had feared; her husband forgot what he had come to buy. Mrs. Pepperpot shouted at the top of her voice, 'MACARONI!', but it was impossible to get him to hear.

'A quarter of a pound of coffee, please,' said her husband.

'Anything else?' asked the grocer.

'MACARONI!' shouted Mrs. Pepperpot.

'Two pounds of sugar,' said her husband.

'Anything more?'

'MACARONI!' shouted Mrs. Pepperpot.

But at last her husband remembered the macaroni of his own accord. The grocer hurriedly filled a bag. He thought he felt something move, but he didn't say a word.

'That's all, thank you,' said Mr. Pepperpot. When he got outside the door he was just about to make sure his

wife was still in his pocket when a van drew up and offered to give him a lift all the way home. Once there he took off his knapsack with all the shopping in it and put his hand in his pocket to lift out his wife.

The pocket was empty.

Now he was really frightened. First he thought she was teasing him, but when he had called three times and still no wife appeared, he put on his hat again and hurried back to the shop.

The grocer saw him coming. 'He's probably going to complain about the mouse in the macaroni,' he thought.

'Have you forgotten anything, Mr. Pepperpot?' he asked, and smiled as pleasantly as he could.

Mr. Pepperpot was looking all round. 'Yes,' he said.

'I would be very grateful, Mr. Pepperpot, if you would keep it to yourself about the mouse being in the macaroni. I'll let you have these fine blue coffee cups if you'll say no more about it.'

'Mouse?' Mr. Pepperpot looked puzzled.

'Shh!' said the grocer, and hurriedly started wrapping up the cups.

Then Mr. Pepperpot realized that the grocer had mistaken his wife for a mouse. So he took the cups and rushed home as fast as he could. By the time he got there he was in a sweat of fear that his wife might have been squeezed to death in the macaroni bag.

'Oh, my dear wife,' he muttered to himself. 'My poor darling wife. I'll never again be ashamed of you being the size of a pepperpot—as long as you're still alive!'

When he opened the door she was standing by the cooking-stove, dishing up the macaroni—as large as life; in fact, as large as you or I.

Queen of the Crows

DID you know that the woman who was as small as a pepperpot was queen of all the crows in the forest?

No, of course you didn't, because it was a secret between Mrs. Pepperpot and me until now. But now I'm going to tell you how it happened.

Outside the old woman's house there was a wooden fence and on it used to sit a large crow.

'I can't understand why that crow has to sit there staring in at the kitchen window all the time,' said Mr. Pepperpot.

'I can't imagine,' said Mrs. Pepperpot. 'Shoo! Get along with you!'

But the crow didn't move from the fence.

Then one day Mrs. Pepperpot had her shrinking turn again (I can't remember now what she was supposed to be doing that day, but she was very busy), and by the time she had clambered over the doorstep she was quite out of breath.

'Oh dear, it's certainly hard to be so small,' she puffed.

Suddenly there was a sound of flapping wings and the

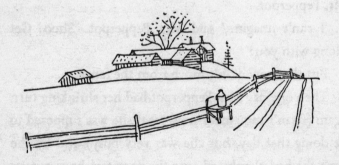

crow swooped down, picked up Mrs. Pepperpot by her skirt and flew up over the highest fir trees in the forest with her.

'What's the idea, may I ask? You wait till I'm back to my proper size and I'll beat you with my birch rod and chase you off for good!'

'Caw-caw! You're small enough now, at any rate,' said the crow; 'I've waited a long time for this. I saw you turn small once before, you see, so I thought it might happen again. And here we are, but only just in time. Today is the Crows' Festival and *I'm* to be Queen of the Crows!'

'If you're to be Queen of the Crows, you surely don't need to take an old woman like me along?'

'That's just where you're wrong,' said the crow, and flapped her wings; the old woman was heavier than she had expected. 'Wait till we get back to my nest, then you'll see why.'

'There's not much else I *can* do,' thought poor Mrs. Pepperpot as she dangled from the crow's claws.

'Here we are; home!' said the crow, and dropped Mrs. Pepperpot into the nest. 'Lucky it's empty.'

'It certainly is; I fell right on a spiky twig and grazed my shinbone.'

'Poor little thing!' said the crow. 'But look, I've made you a lovely bed of feathers and down. You'll find the down very snug and warm, and the feathers are just the thing when night falls and the wind begins to blow.'

'What do I want with feathers and down?'

'I want you to lie down and go to sleep,' said the crow. 'But first you must lend me your clothes. So please take off your head-scarf now, and your blouse and your skirt.

'The scarf I want you to tie round my neck, the skirt goes on one wing and the blouse on the other. Then I shall fly to the clearing in the forest where all the crows are meeting for the Festival. The finest-looking crow will be chosen queen, and that's going to be me! When I win I'll think of you. Caw-caw!'

'Well, if you think you'll be any better looking in my old clothes, you're welcome,' said Mrs. Pepperpot as she dressed up the crow.

'Hurry, hurry!' said the crow. 'There's another crow living over there in that fir tree on the hill. She'll be dropping in here on her way; we were going to the Festival together. But now that I'm all dressed up I'd rather go alone. Caw-caw-caw!' And off she flew.

Mrs. Pepperpot sat shivering in her petticoat, but then she thought of burrowing deep under the feathers and down as the crow had told her to do, and she found she was soon warm and cosy.

Suddenly the whole branch started swaying, and on the end perched a huge crow.

'Mary Crow, are you at home?' croaked the crow, sidling up and poking her big beak over the edge of the nest.

'Mary Crow has gone to the Festival,' said Mrs. Pepperpot.

'Then who are you, who are you?' asked the crow.

'I'm just an old woman shivering with cold, because Mary Crow has borrowed my clothes.'

'Caw-caw! Oh blow! She'll be the finest-looking crow at the Festival,' shrieked the crow as she threw herself into the air from the branch. 'But I'll have the scarf off her!'

Mrs. Pepperpot lay down to sleep again. Suddenly she rolled right over into the corner of the nest, the branch was shaking so much.

'That'll be another crow,' she thought, and quite right, it was; the biggest crow she had ever seen was swinging on the tip of the branch.

'Mary Crow, Mary Crow, have you seen Betty Crow?'

'I've seen both Mary Crow *and* Betty Crow,' said Mrs. Pepperpot.

'Who are you, who are you?' squawked the crow.

'I'm just an old woman shivering with cold because Mary Crow has borrowed my clothes.'

'Caw-caw! What a bore! Now Mary Crow will be the best-looking crow.'

'I'm not so sure about that,' said the old woman, 'because Betty Crow flew after Mary Crow and was going to have the scarf off her.'

'I'll take the skirt, I'll take the skirt!' croaked the biggest crow, and took off from the branch with such a bound that Mrs. Pepperpot had to hold on tight not to get thrown out of the nest.

In the clearing in the forest there were lots and lots of crows. They sat round in a circle and, one by one, they hopped into the middle to show themselves. Some of the crows could hop on one leg without touching the ground with their wings. Others had different kinds of tricks, and the crows sitting round had to choose the best one to be their queen.

At last there were only three crows left. They sat well away from each other, polishing their feathers and looking very fierce indeed. One had a scarf, the second had a skirt and the third had a blouse. So you can guess which crows *they* were. One of them was to be chosen queen.

'The crow with the scarf round her neck is the best,' said some of the crows, 'she looks most like a human being.'

'No, no; the crow with the skirt looks best!'

'Not at all! The crow with the blouse looks most dignified, and a queen should be dignified.'

Suddenly something fell with a bump to the ground; the jay had arrived right in the middle of the Festival with a strange-looking bird in its beak.

'Caw-caw! The jay has no business to be here!' croaked all the crows.

'I won't stay a minute,' said the jay. 'I've just brought you your queen!' and he flew off.

All the crows stared at the strange little raggedy bird in the middle of the ring. They could see it was covered in crow's feathers and down, but raggedy crows could not be allowed at the Festival.

'It's against the law!' said the biggest crow.

'Let's peck it, let's peck it!' said Mary Crow.

'Yes, let's hack it to pieces!' said Betty Crow.

'Yes, yes!' croaked all the crows. 'We can't have raggedy birds here!'

'Wait a minute!' said the raggedy bird, and climbed on to a tree-stump. 'I'll sing you a song.' And before they could stop it, it started singing 'Who Killed Cock Robin?' And it knew all the verses. The crows were delighted; they clapped and flapped their wings till the raggedy bird lost nearly all its feathers.

'D'you know any more? D'you know any more?' they croaked.

'I can dance the polka,' said the raggedy bird, and danced round the circle till they were all out of breath.

'You shall be our Queen!' they all shouted. 'Four Court Crows will carry you wherever you wish to go.'

'How wonderful!' laughed the Queen of the Crows. 'Then they must carry me to the house over there by the edge of the forest.'

'What would Your Majesty like to wear?'

'I would like to wear a skirt, a blouse and a head-scarf,' said the Queen.

Much later that night there was a knock at the cottage door. Mr. Pepperpot opened it, and there stood his wife.

'You're very late, wife,' he said. 'Where have you been?'

'I've been to a Festival,' she answered.

'But why are you covered in feathers?'

'You just go to bed and don't trouble yourself,' said Mrs. Pepperpot. She went over and stuck a feather in the corner of the window.

'Why do you do that?' asked her husband.

'For no reason at all.'

But she really did it because she had been chosen Queen of the Crows.

Mrs. Pepperpot at the bazaar

ONE day Mrs. Pepperpot was alone in her kitchen. At least, she was not *quite* alone, because Hannah, the little girl who had had the doll for Christmas, was there as well. She was busy scraping out a bowl and licking the spoon, for the old woman had been making gingerbread shapes.

There was a knock at the door. Mrs. Pepperpot said, 'Come in.' And in walked three very smart ladies.

'Good afternoon,' said the smart ladies. 'We are collecting prizes for the lottery at the school bazaar this evening. Do you think you have some little thing we could have? The money from the bazaar is for the boys' brass band—they need new instruments.'

'Oh, I'd like to help with that,' said Mrs. Pepperpot, for she dearly loved brass bands. 'Would a plate of gingerbread be any use?'

'Of course,' said the smart ladies, but they laughed behind her back. 'We could take it with us now if you have it ready,' they said. But Mrs. Pepperpot wanted to go to the bazaar herself, so she said she would bring the gingerbread.

So the three smart ladies went away and Mrs. Pepperpot was very proud and pleased that she was going to a bazaar.

Hannah was still scraping away at the bowl and licking the sweet mixture from the spoon.

'May I come with you?' she asked.

'Certainly, if your father and mother will let you.'

'I'm sure they will,' said the child, 'because Father has to work at the factory and Mother is at her sewing all day.'

'Be here at six o'clock then,' said Mrs. Pepperpot, and started making another batch of gingerbread shapes.

But when Hannah came back at six the old woman was not there. All the doors were open, so she went from room to room, calling her. When she got back to the kitchen she heard an odd noise coming from the table. The mixing bowl was upside down, so she lifted it carefully. And there underneath sat her friend who was now again as small as a pepperpot.

'Isn't this a nuisance?' said Mrs. Pepperpot. 'I was just cleaning out the bowl after putting the gingerbread in the oven when I suddenly started shrinking. Then the bowl turned over on me. Quick! Get the cakes out of the oven before they burn!'

But it was too late; the gingerbread was burnt to a cinder.

Mrs. Pepperpot sat down and cried, she was so disappointed. But she soon gave that up and started thinking instead. Suddenly she laughed out loud and said:

'Hannah! Put me under the tap and give me a good wash. We're going to the bazaar, you and I!'

'But you can't go to the bazaar like that!' said Hannah.

'Oh yes, I can,' said Mrs. Pepperpot, 'as long as you do what I say.'

Hannah promised, but Mrs. Pepperpot gave her some very queer orders. First she was to fetch a silk ribbon and tie it round the old woman so that it looked like a skirt. Then she was to fetch some tinsel from the Christmas decorations. This she had to wind round and round to make a silver bodice. And lastly she had to make a bonnet of gold foil.

'Now you must wrap me carefully in cellophane and put me in a cardboard box,' said Mrs. Pepperpot.

'Why?' asked Hannah.

'When I've promised them a prize for the bazaar they must have it,' said Mrs. Pepperpot, 'so I'm giving them myself. Just put me down on one of the tables and say you've brought a mechanical doll. Tell them you keep the key in your pocket and then pretend to wind me up so that people can see how clever I am.'

Hannah did as she was told, and when she got to the

bazaar and put the wonderful doll on the table, many people clapped their hands and crowded round to see.

'What a pretty doll!' they said. 'And what a lovely dress!'

'Look at her gold bonnet!'

Mrs. Pepperpot lay absolutely still in her cardboard box, but when she heard how everybody praised her, she winked at Hannah with one eye, and Hannah knew what she wanted. She lifted Mrs. Pepperpot very carefully out of the box and pretended to wind her up at the back with a key.

Everyone was watching her. But when Mrs. Pepperpot began walking across the table, picking her way through the prizes, there was great excitement.

'Look, the doll can walk!'

And when Mrs. Pepperpot began to dance they started shouting and yelling with delight, 'The doll is dancing!'

The three smart ladies who had been to see Mrs. Pepperpot earlier in the day sat in special seats and looked very grand. One of them had given six expensive coffee cups, the second an elegant table mat and the third a beautiful iced layer cake.

Mrs. Pepperpot decided to go over and speak to them, for she was afraid they had recognized her and thought it queer that she hadn't brought the gingerbread.

The three smart ladies were very pleased when the doll came walking across the table to them.

'Come to me!' said the one who had given the coffee cups, and stretched her hand out towards Mrs. Pepperpot, who walked on to it obediently.

'Let me hold her a little,' said the lady with the elegant table mat, and Mrs. Pepperpot went over to her hand.

'Now it's my turn,' said the lady with the iced cake.

'I'm sure they know it's me,' thought Mrs. Pepperpot, 'that's why they stare at me so hard and hold me on their hands.'

But then the lady with the cake said, 'Well, I must say, this is a much better prize than the gingerbread that the odd old woman offered us today.'

Now she should never have said that; Mrs. Pepperpot leaped straight out of her hand and landed PLOP! right in the middle of the beautiful iced layer cake. Then she got up and waded right through it. The cake lady screamed, but people were shouting with laughter by now.

'Take that doll away!' shrieked the second lady, but *squish, squash!* went Mrs. Pepperpot's sticky feet, right across her lovely table mat.

'Get that dreadful doll away!' cried the third lady. But it was too late; Mrs. Pepperpot was on the tray with

the expensive coffee cups, and began to dance a jig. Cups and saucers flew about and broke in little pieces.

What a-to-do! The conductor of the brass band had quite a job to quieten them all down. He announced that the winning numbers of the lottery would be given out.

'First prize will be the wonderful mechanical doll,' he said.

When Hannah heard that she was very frightened. What would happen if somebody won Mrs. Pepperpot, so that she couldn't go home to her husband? She tugged at Mrs. Pepperpot's skirt and whispered, 'Shall I put you in my pocket and creep away?'

'No,' said Mrs. Pepperpot.

'But think how awful it would be if someone won you and took you home.'

'What must be must be!' said Mrs. Pepperpot.

The conductor called out the winning number, '311!' Everyone looked at their tickets, but no one had number 311.

'That's a good thing!' sighed Hannah with relief. There would have to be another draw. But just then she remembered she had a ticket in her hand; it was number 311!

'Wait!' she cried, and showed her ticket. The conductor looked at it and saw it was the right one.

So Hannah was allowed to take Mrs. Pepperpot home.

Next day the old woman was her proper size again and Hannah only a little girl, and Mrs. Pepperpot said, 'You're my little girl, aren't you?'

'Yes,' said Hannah, 'and you're my very own Mrs. Pepperpot, because I won you at the bazaar yesterday.'

And that was the end of Mrs. Pepperpot's adventures for a very long time.

Mr. Puffblow's hat

THERE was once a man called Mr. Puffblow who had an enormous hat. Mr. Puffblow was a very severe sort of man, and when he walked down the street he used to get very angry indeed if any of the children stared at his hat. And if they as much as stopped and looked at the house where he lived he would rush out and chase them off, because he thought they wanted to steal his apples.

Nobody dared go against Mr. Puffblow. 'Ssh!' mothers would say to their children playing in the street. 'You'd better be quiet—Mr. Puffblow is coming this way!'

Every day at precisely half past eleven Mr. Puffblow walked down the street to fetch his pint of milk from the dairy. So, until *that* was over, everybody stayed indoors.

One day the West Wind came tearing through the town, and I don't think there is anything like the West Wind for upsetting things in the autumn; the mischief it gets up to is nobody's business.

Now suddenly the West Wind caught sight of Mr.

Puffblow walking down the street with his enormous
hat on.

'Wheee!' said the West Wind. 'That's just the hat for
me!'

So, with a puff and a blow, it tipped Mr. Puffblow's
hat off his head.

The hat bowled along the pavement. Mr. Puffblow
ran after it. But just as he was about to catch it, the West
Wind pounced and blew it further away. This game went
on for a long time until at last the West Wind carried
the hat high up into the air, right over the rooftops of
the town to the wood beyond.

'I'm tired of playing with you now,' said the West

Wind to the hat. 'I'm going to drop you in this brook and leave you to sink or swim. Good luck!'

The hat turned two more somersaults in the air, then plopped into the brook and floated away like a little round ship.

It so happened that a tiny fieldmouse had been out in the wood that day gathering nuts, and he had fallen into the brook. He could swim all right, but the current was so strong he was almost drowned struggling against it.

When he saw the hat sailing past he caught hold of the brim with his paws and clambered up to the top of the crown.

'This would make a very good ship,' thought the

fieldmouse. 'I wish some of the other mice could see me now.' And he gave a loud squeak.

Sure enough, another fieldmouse heard him, and when he saw the fine-looking ship he called the other mice, and in the end there were eight little fieldmice sailing along on the hat. The one who got on first was the captain, the second was his mate and the rest were the crew.

You have no idea what fun those fieldmice had with Mr. Puffblow's hat that autumn! Every day they went for a sail, and when winter came and it got too cold, they dragged the hat on to dry land and used it for a house. All through the winter they sat inside it, snug and warm, telling each other mouse fairy-tales and singing mouse carols at Christmas.

And when spring came they started sailing again.

Then one day there was a great noise and to-do in the wood. A whole crowd of children from the town were out for a picnic. There was a man with them and they were all laughing and shouting and having a fine time together. The man carried the smallest one on his shoulders while the others were clinging to his coat-tails. They picked flowers for him and showed him all the nicest things they could find in the wood on a spring day.

Suddenly they stopped by the brook. 'Look over there!' cried one of the children. 'Look at that big hat on the other bank!'

The mice had just dragged the hat out of the brook because they were going home to supper.

When the man saw the hat he laughed and laughed. Because, you see, he knew it.

Can you guess who he was? Mr. Puffblow! But a very much nicer Mr. Puffblow now, and do you know why? Well, when he used to wear that enormous hat on his head he was always afraid the children would laugh at him. But from the moment he lost the hat he became quite different; he was no longer afraid.

'There's your old hat, Mr. Puffblow!' shouted the children with glee. 'Don't you want to wear it again?'

'Certainly not!' said Mr. Puffblow. 'Come along now, children, let's pick anemones.'

So they did.

And the fieldmice are using Mr. Puffblow's hat for a ship to this day.

Miriam-from-America

THERE was once a doll who was so beautifully smart that she had to sit all day, every day, on top of a chest of drawers. She couldn't *do* anything, not even shut her eyes or stand on her feet, and her fine silk dress was sewn on to her body, so she couldn't be undressed. But there was no doubt about it; she was the grandest of all the dolls just because she sat on top of the chest of drawers.

The little girl who owned the doll never allowed her school friends to touch her. When they asked why they mustn't touch her, the little girl said:

'Don't you know that this doll is called Miriam and comes from America? What's more, she's crossed the Atlantic in a ship, and even *I*'m not allowed to touch her till I'm a big girl.'

When her friends heard this their eyes grew round with astonishment and, putting their hands behind their backs, they stood and stared at Miriam-from-America.

One day the window near the chest of drawers stood

open, and someone opened the door as well so that there was a draught. This blew Miriam off the chest straight out of the window into the garden below. There she lay, quite still, looking up at the sky.

It grew darker and darker, until it was late night and the stars began to twinkle. All at once, the full moon came sailing across the sky.

'What is that strange-looking thing in the garden?' said the moon, and turned his light on Miriam.

Miriam said nothing; she just went on lying there. But the wind whistled in the tree tops and answered for her: 'That is Miriam-from-America. She is the most elegant doll because she usually sits right on top of a chest of drawers.'

'Can't she speak for herself?' asked the moon.

'I don't think so,' said the wind. 'Can you talk, Miriam?'

Miriam said nothing.

'Try and talk to us—just a little,' said the moon.

Miriam still didn't move, but the moon saw she wanted to say something, so he waited.

'Over the sea and under the sky!' Miriam said suddenly.

'Why do you say "over the sea and under the sky"?' asked the moon.

'Because I have sailed over the sea,' said Miriam, 'and I thought that was great fun. And now I'm lying under the sky and that is even more fun.'

'But I suppose sitting on a chest of drawers being the most elegant, the most beautiful, doll is more fun still?' said the wind.

'It's the dullest thing in the world!' said Miriam. 'Couldn't you two help me so that I don't have to be so elegant, so smart, any more?'

'That's easy,' said the wind, and blew Miriam straight into a big puddle. Miriam laughed; it was lovely to splash about in water. She had never tried that before.

'I must help too,' said the moon, and he threw a beam of light on the kennel where the dog Rover lay asleep. He woke up at once and saw Miriam lying in the puddle. So he took her smart silk dress between his

teeth and ran down the road with her. Miriam was jolted up and down, but she didn't mind a bit because she knew Rover well; she had often seen him from her chest of drawers when he lay curled up by the fire. And now here she was, having a lovely game with him!

The moon followed them down the street, and so did the wind, turning somersaults all the way. At last they came back to the house where Miriam lived. But how was she to get indoors again? The window was still open but Miriam couldn't possibly climb up to it.

'We shall have to ask the crow to carry her up in his beak,' said the moon. So they did. The crow was very ready to help. He flew through the window with Miriam and set her down on the chest of drawers.

Well, you can imagine the fuss there was next day when the little girl's mother saw what a mess Miriam was in! But the little girl was very pleased, because from now on she could play with Miriam as much as she liked. She took her for rides in the doll's pram, and every time the wind blew Miriam waved her hand—just a little bit. This was supposed to mean:

'Thank you, wind, for helping me get away from the chest of drawers!'

Jumping Jack and his friends

THE things I am going to tell you about in this story only happened last night. They happened after everyone had gone to bed; not only the little children and the big children, but the grown-ups as well.

In a shed—an ordinary kind of garden shed which people use for bicycles and shovels and rakes and spades —lived a family of toys.

There was a tricycle, a skipping rope hanging on a nail and two hop-scotch stones stuck in a crack in the floor. Almost hidden, stood a little red wheelbarrow which the children used in the sand pit, and in it lay a ball and a jumping jack. This jumping jack was so smart he had his name painted across his back in big letters: JUMPING JACK.

The toys had been in the shed all winter. They had seen the snowdrifts when the grown-ups came for shovels to clear the paths, and they had heard the wind howl and sigh. But just lately the toys had heard a new noise—a slow *drip . . . drip . . .* from the roof. Then it had turned into *drippy-drippy-drop* and at last a very quick *drip,*

drip, drip, drip, and they knew that all the snow had melted from the roof.

'Are we going out now?' asked Jumping Jack, who had never seen winter before.

'Not for a long time yet,' answered the Wheelbarrow.

One day a little boy came for the Tricycle. He got on it and pedalled out into the spring sunshine, ringing his bell loudly.

'Will it be our turn next?' asked Jumping Jack.

'Not yet,' said the Wheelbarrow.

Then a little girl, whose name was Cathy, came into the shed. 'Look, there's my ball!' she shouted, and hugged the Ball tightly. But it sagged and made a hissing noise because it had a split in its rubber tummy.

'Oh, you horrid Ball!' Cathy cried, and threw it back in the Wheelbarrow. Instead she took the Skipping Rope and ran out with it into the sunshine. She jumped and skipped so hard her hair stood out like a halo round her head.

'Why didn't she take the Ball with her?' asked Jumping Jack. But the Wheelbarrow only said 'Hmm.' It didn't want to be unkind to the poor Ball.

Nothing more was said. But a few days later they could hear a bouncing noise outside the shed; *bump-bump* it went against the wall, and the Wheelbarrow knew what that meant. So did the Old Ball; it lay there sighing through its crack all day long.

The Wheelbarrow thought about this for a long time —several days and nights. Then last night, after everyone had gone to bed, as I said, it gave a wooden creak and said to the Old Ball:

'I think it's a shame you're never to go out in the sunshine again. And I'm sorry to have to be the one to tell you, but you do understand, don't you, that Cathy has got a new ball and she's forgotten about you?'

'Yes,' sighed the Old Ball.

'I don't think Peter has forgotten *me*,' said Jumping Jack; 'he made such a fuss of me last summer. Anyway, it was just a mistake my being put out here in the shed. It was the charlady who carried all the summer toys out here when the snow came, and she didn't notice I'd got mixed up with them. I've been jumping mad ever since!'

'There's no need to get hoity-toity and stick your nose in the air even if you were only made last summer. You never know how long you will last. I've seen many jumping jacks in my time. They're fine as long as the strings don't break and both arms and legs are working. But sooner or later something gets broken and that's the end of that. . . . Well, not always, of course!' he added quickly when he saw that Jumping Jack looked quite frightened and ready to cry.

'I'm not at all perfect myself,' the Wheelbarrow went on. 'There's a weakness in one of my arms. The carpenter, who made me, put a thick layer of paint over the crack, so that it wouldn't show. But I've often been afraid when Peter filled me up with sand. Last year, I almost broke several times, so I don't think he'll use me again when summer comes along.'

'What a shame!' wheezed the Old Ball. He was sorry for the Wheelbarrow, but pleased at the same time that he wouldn't be left all alone in the dark shed.

'Then it's just me who is going out in the sunshine,' said Jumping Jack in a cheeky sort of way.

'You ought to be ashamed of yourself!' said the Wheelbarrow. 'We're all in the same boat—or rather, you and the Old Ball are in the same barrow, and that barrow happens to be me. And now I'm going to tell you what we're going to do—we three.'

'Do? What can we three do?' asked Jumping Jack.

'Listen. A long time ago there was an old wheelbarrow in here which told me that a night would come
when all old broken or unwanted toys would come to
life and go off and find new homes for themselves. I've
been waiting for that night ever since, and now tonight
I really think it's come, for I feel a sort of twitching and
tingling in my wheel as if it wants to run. Yes, I'm sure
we must be off!'

'But I don't want to go with you!' shouted Jumping
Jack, 'I want to stay with Peter. I want to go back to the
nursery with all the other toys; I don't want to go to a
new home!'

But before he could say any more the Wheelbarrow

lifted his arms and rolled out of the shed with the Old
Ball and Jumping Jack. The wheel creaked, the Old Ball
sighed and Jumping Jack's arms and legs were tossing to
and fro, so that it looked as if he was trying to get out,
which, of course, was what he *wanted* to do. But the
Wheelbarrow just went steadily on, balancing on one
wheel.

Soon they met other toys; first a tricycle with crooked

handlebars which lurched from one side of the road to the other and nearly ran over them.

'Good evening,' said the Wheelbarrow.

'I think you should say "Good night" when it's so late,' said the Tricycle. 'I don't know why, but I had such an awful itch in my pedals, I just had to come out on to the road. And now I don't know where I'm going. . . .' And he was off, lurching from side to side.

After a while they met a doll with only one arm.

'Good night!' said the Wheelbarrow, for he was not going to make the same mistake twice.

'Good night!' said the Doll as she danced and pranced in her pink knitted slippers.

'Where are you going?' the Wheelbarrow called after her.

'I don't know. And I don't know where I come from. I just know I have to keep on and on!'

'Why couldn't she have come with us?' asked Jumping Jack, when she had disappeared.

'Stupid!' said the Barrow. 'Don't you understand that the whole idea is that each toy should go to a different home? If one child gets a whole lot of old broken toys the same thing will happen again—some of them will be thrown away. No, each child is to have *one* toy.' And they rolled on.

They met many queer toys.

A skipping rope came waving along the road, and after it a humming-top, tripping and bumping over the stones in the road. A very small toy train came chuffing along at full speed. It headed straight for the ditch and disappeared under the water. But a moment later—*bubble-bubble, bubble-bubble, whoosh!*—up it came on the other side and ran straight into a wooden hoop which was bowling in the opposite direction. The hoop fell over, the train fell over, but that didn't worry them; they were up and off again before you could count three. A teddy-bear with a split down the back came plodding by. All he needed was a bit more sawdust stuffing and a few stitches, and some little girl would be glad to have him and mend his back.

After a time the Old Ball started rolling about in the barrow in a restless sort of way: 'I say, Wheelbarrow, can you stop a minute? There's a little cottage up there by the wood; something tells me I have to get off here.'

The Wheelbarrow stopped to let the Old Ball roll off, and it bounced up on the cottage window to look in. Sure enough there was a little girl asleep in bed clutching an old rag doll.

'This must be the place all right,' said the Old Ball. 'Thanks for bringing me along and for being so kind to me. I'll just stay here on the doorstep, then she's sure to find me in the morning. Goodbye!'

The Wheelbarrow and Jumping Jack said goodbye and rolled on until the Barrow suddenly said, 'I can feel a sort of pull inside me; I think we have to turn up this little path through the wood.'

So they did. There was still a bit of snow here and there, making the wheel go *crunch*, *crunch*.

At last they came to a clearing with an even smaller

cottage than the one where the Old Ball had stopped. The snow lay in drifts against the windows, so the Wheelbarrow took a run at one of them and managed to get high enough to look in. And there was a little boy asleep. By the stove stood a box with a string tied to it. That was all *he* had in the way of a wheelbarrow.

'There, I *thought* so!' said the Wheelbarrow. 'This is the place for me. But what about you, Jack? Haven't *you* felt anything yet? Haven't you had an itch in those long arms and legs of yours as if somebody was pulling your string?'

'No, I haven't!' said Jumping Jack very crossly. 'I'm

not broken, that's why. It's only the broken and cast-off toys who have to find new homes; I have Peter to love me at home, and I don't know why you brought me along—especially when I shouted to you to let me off, you stupid old bundle of sticks!'

'It wasn't my fault. Just when you wanted to get out, something told me to start off and take you with me, so I did.'

Then suddenly the Barrow *knew* why he had brought Jack along. 'Don't you understand? You had to see for yourself what happens tonight, so that you can go home and tell all the other toys. You must tell them they needn't worry even if they do get broken. There are lots of children who will have them and mend them too, so that they're as good as new.'

And all at once Jumping Jack could see it too. 'You're quite right,' he said.

And then he found, to his surprise, that he could move. What fun it was to stretch his legs and arms without being jerked by the string! He hopped first on one leg, then the other, and then he turned complete somersaults. Then he thanked the Wheelbarrow for his trip and said goodbye.

After that, with his string floating straight out behind him like a tail, he ran and ran till he reached the little shed in the garden at home.

And now Jumping Jack has been waiting all day for it to grow dark; for not until the children are in bed and asleep can he go out and give his message to all the broken and unwanted toys.

*　　*　　*　　*　　*

So if you wake up tomorrow morning and find that your old doll seems to be smiling just a little, or that your chipped trumpet sounds better than it has for a long time, that will be because Jumping Jack has told them about the trip he made with his friends the Wheelbarrow and the Old Ball last night.

The potato with big ideas

THERE was once a potato which lay waiting for someone to come and dig it up. The other potatoes were just

quietly growing larger and larger, but this particular potato had ideas; he was stuck-up. And he was bored with waiting.

'Hi, everybody!' the stuck-up potato said. 'I'm not

going to wait any longer. I'll try to get out of this hole by myself. People must be longing to see what a beautiful potato I am; everything that is beautiful must see the light of day and enjoy the sunshine. Here I come! The most beautiful potato in all the world!'

You may know that all potatoes are tied to the mother potato by a thin thread (so that she can keep them in order, no doubt). Now that stuck-up potato began tugging at his thread, and the thread stretched and stretched till one fine day the stuck-up potato found himself lying on the ground above.

'Hurrah, hurrah! Here I am at last! Good morning, Mr. Weed! Good morning, Mrs. Worm! I am the world's most beautiful potato. And if you, Mr. Sun, would like to shine on me for a moment, you can.'

'With the greatest of pleasure,' answered the sun, 'but it won't be good for you, you know.'

'Who cares? You just shine away and let me enjoy a nice hot sun-bath.'

So the sun shone on that stuck-up potato and turned him blue, green, red and purple all over. This made the potato more pleased with himself than ever:

'When the boys come past and see me lying here they will say: "My goodness! What a fine potato! We must take that home to Mother for dinner." And one of them will put me carefully in his pocket. When his mother sees me she will say: "Goodness gracious! What a wonderful potato; it's much too good for me. I will give it to the parson." And when the parson sees me he will say: "Goodness gracious! My, oh my! What a marvellous potato; I'll give it to the bishop." And when the bishop sees me he will say: "Goodness gracious! My, oh my! And bless my soul! But what an exquisite potato. I must send it straight to the Pope in Rome." Then I will be wrapped in silver paper and sent to the Pope. And when the Pope sees me he will put on his finest clothes and sit on his best silver throne and put me on a gold plate and eat me, while all the church bells ring to tell the world that now the Pope is eating the most beautiful potato from Puddlington-on-the-Marsh.'

But just as the potato was having this lovely dream, the farmer and his wife and their little boy came out into the field to start lifting the potatoes.

They sang as they worked, and shouted to each other every time they found a really whacking big potato.

'Wait till they see *me*, then they'll have something to crow about!' thought the stuck-up potato.

Suddenly the little boy shouted: 'Look at this funny-looking potato! It's blue and red and green all over!'

'Throw it in the pig-bucket,' said his father; 'you can't eat that sort. It's been on top of the earth instead of underneath, where it should have been. But the pigs won't mind what colour it is.'

And so that stuck-up potato ended his days in the pig-trough instead of on a gold plate in the Pope's palace in Rome, which all goes to show that even if you have big ideas it's sometimes wiser to leave them alone.

The mice and the Christmas tree

Now you shall hear the story about a family of mice who lived behind the larder wall.

*   *   *   *   *

Every Christmas Eve, Mother Mouse and the children swept and dusted their whole house with their tails, and for a Christmas tree Father Mouse decorated an old boot with spider's web instead of tinsel. For Christmas presents, the children were each given a little nut, and Mother Mouse held up a piece of bacon fat for them all to sniff.

After that, they danced round and round the boot, and sang and played games till they were tired out. Then

Father Mouse would say: 'That's all for tonight! Time to go to bed!'

That is how it had been every Christmas and that is how it was to be this year. The little mice held each other by the tail and danced round the boot, while Granny Mouse enjoyed the fun from her rocking-chair, which wasn't a rocking-chair at all, but a small turnip.

But when Father Mouse said, 'That's all for tonight! Time to go to bed!' all the children dropped each other's tails and shouted: 'No! No!'

'What's that?' said Father Mouse. 'When I say it's time for bed, it's time for bed!'

'We don't want to go!' cried the children, and hid behind Granny's turnip rocking-chair.

'What's all this nonsense?' said Mother Mouse. 'Christmas is over now, so off you go, the lot of you!'

'No, no!' wailed the children, and climbed on to Granny's knee. She hugged them all lovingly. 'Why don't you want to go to bed, my little sugar lumps?'

'Because we want to go upstairs to the big drawing-

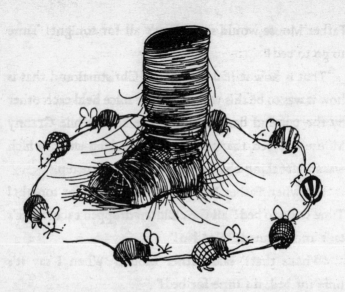

room and dance round a proper Christmas tree,' said the eldest Mouse child. 'You see, I've been peeping through a crack in the wall and I saw a huge Christmas tree with lots and lots of lights on it.'

'We want to see the Christmas tree and all the lights too!' shouted the other children.

'Oh, but the drawing-room can be a very dangerous place for mice,' said Granny.

'Not when all the people have gone to bed,' objected the eldest Mouse child.

'Oh, do let's go!' they all pleaded.

Mother and Father Mouse didn't know what to say, but they couldn't very well disappoint the children on Christmas Eve.

'Perhaps we could take them up there just for a minute or two,' suggested Mother Mouse.

'Very well,' said Father, 'but follow me closely.'

So they set off. They tiptoed past three tins of herring, two large jars of honey and a barrel of cider.

'We have to go very carefully here,' whispered Father Mouse, 'not to knock over any bottles. Are you all right, Granny?'

'Of course I'm all right,' said Granny, 'you just carry on. I haven't been up in the drawing-room since I was a little Mouse girl; it'll be fun to see it all again.'

'Mind the trap!' said the eldest Mouse child. 'It's behind that sack of potatoes.'

'I know that,' said Granny; 'it's been there since I was

a child. I'm not afraid of that!' And she took a flying leap right over the trap and scuttled after the others up the wall.

'What a lovely tree!' cried all the children when they peeped out of the hole by the drawing-room fireplace. 'But where are the lights? You said there'd be lots and lots of lights, didn't you? Didn't you?' The children shouted, crowding round the eldest one, who was quite sure there had been lights the day before.

They stood looking for a little while. Then suddenly a whole lot of coloured lights lit up the tree! Do you know what had happened? By accident, Granny had touched the electric switch by the fireplace.

'Oh, how lovely!' they all exclaimed, and Father and Mother and Granny thought it was very nice too. They walked right round the tree, looking at the decorations, the little paper baskets, the glass balls and the glittering tinsel garlands. But the children found something even more exciting: a mechanical lorry!

Of course, they couldn't wind it up themselves, but its young master had wound it up before he went to bed, to be ready for him to play with in the morning. So when the Mouse children clambered into it, it started off right away.

'Children, children! You mustn't make such a noise!' warned Mother Mouse.

But the children didn't listen; they were having a wonderful time going round and round and round in the lorry.

'As long as the cat doesn't come!' said Father Mouse anxiously.

He had hardly spoken before the cat walked silently through the open door.

Father, Mother and Granny Mouse all made a dash for the hole in the skirting but the children were trapped in the lorry, which just went on going round and round and round. They had never been so scared in all their Mouse lives.

The cat crouched under the tree, and every time the lorry passed she tried to tap it with her front paw. But it was going too fast and she missed.

Then the lorry started slowing down. 'I think we'd better make a jump for it and try to get up in the tree,' said the eldest Mouse. So when the lorry stopped they all gave a big jump and landed on the branches of the tree.

One hid in a paper basket, another behind a bulb (which nearly burned him), a third swung on a glass ball and the fourth rolled himself up in some cotton wool. But where was the eldest Mouse? Oh yes, he had climbed right to the top and was balancing next to the star and shouting at the cat:

'Silly, silly cat,
You can't catch us!
You're much too fat,
Silly, silly cat!'

But the cat pretended not to hear or see the little mice. She sharpened her claws on the lorry. 'I'm not interested in catching mice tonight,' she said as if to herself, 'I've been waiting for a chance to play with this lorry all day.'

'Pooh! That's just a story!' said the eldest who was also the bravest. 'You'd catch us quick enough if we came down.'

'No, I wouldn't. Not on Christmas Eve!' said the cat. And she kept her word. When they did all come timidly down, she never moved, but just said: 'Hurry back to your hole, children. Christmas Eve is the one night when I'm kind to little mice. But woe betide you if I catch you tomorrow morning!'

The little mice pelted through that hole and never stopped running till they got to their home behind the larder wall. There were Father and Mother and Granny Mouse waiting in fear and trembling to know what had happened to them.

When Mother Mouse had heard their story she said, 'You must promise me, children, never to go up to the drawing-room again.'

'We promise! We promise!' they all shouted together.
Then she made them say after her *The Mouse Law*, which
they'd all been taught when they were tiny:

> 'We promise always to obey
> Our parents dear in every way,
> To wipe our feet upon the mat
> And never, never cheek the cat.
>
> Remember too the awful danger
> Of taking money from a stranger;
> We will not go off on our own
> Or give our mother cause to moan.
>
> Odd bits of cheese and bacon-scraps
> Are almost certain to be traps,
> So we must look for bigger things
> Like loaves and cakes and doughnut-rings;
>
> And if these rules we still obey
> We'll live to run another day.'

Never take no for an answer

You see the old woman spinning yarn? She was hard at work one day when a young mouse came out of the hole by the stove.

'Well, well, fancy seeing you,' said the old woman.

'Peep, peep!' said the little mouse. 'My ma sent me to ask what the yarn is for that you're spinning?'

'It's for a jersey for my husband; the one he has is so worn he can't use it any more,' answered the old woman.

'Peep, peep! I'd better go and tell that to my ma!' And the little mouse disappeared down the hole. The old woman went on spinning, but it wasn't long before she heard a scuffling by the stove and there sat the mouse once more.

'You back again?' she asked.

'Peep, peep! My ma said to ask you who is to have your husband's old jersey when he gets the new one?'

'I'm going to use that myself when I milk the cows, because my old milking jacket isn't fit to wear any more,' said the old woman.

'Peep, peep! I'd better go and tell that to my ma,' said the mouse, and he was gone. But in no time at all he was back again.

'What d'you want to know this time?' the old woman asked.

'Peep, peep! My ma wants to know who is to have your old milking jacket when you get your husband's old jersey and he gets the new one?'

'The dog is going to have it in his kennel, because his old rug is so thin it's no good any more.'

'Peep, peep! I'd better go and tell that to my ma,' said the little mouse, and darted away to his hole by the stove. But he had hardly popped in before he popped out again.

'That was quick!' said the woman. 'What is it now?'

'Peep, peep! My ma wants to know who is to have the dog's old rug when he gets your old milking jacket and you get your husband's old jersey and he gets the new one?' said the mouse all in one breath.

'You can have it, if you like,' said the old woman.

'Peep, peep! Thank you *very* much,' said the little mouse. 'Now there'll be an eiderdown for *our* bed as well!' And he was so pleased he sang this song:

'Oh me, oh my!
We'll soon be as snug
As a bug in a rug,
What do you think of that!
Come and see me any time
I'll make you up another rhyme,
But please don't bring the cat.'

Mr. Learn-a-lot and the singing midges

ONE warm summer night Mrs. Midge said to her daughters, 'We'll go and visit Mr. Learn-a-lot, the schoolmaster.'

'What do we want to do that for?' asked the young midges. There were three of them: Big Sister Midge, Middle Sister Midge and Wee Sister Midge.

'We're going to sing to him. You're all so good at singing now, it's a pleasure to listen to you, and Mr. Learn-a-lot is such a good judge of music.'

So they all flew off to Mr. Learn-a-lot's house and hovered outside his bedroom window. Mrs. Midge peered through the glass while her daughters all talked at once in high, squeaky voices:

'Is the window shut, Mama?'

'Won't he open it, Mama?'

'Can't we get in, Mama?'

'I expect he'll open the window when he goes to bed,' said Mrs. Midge.

'He's opening the window now, Mama!'

'Can we go in now, Mama?'

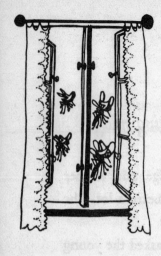

'What shall we sing for him, Mama?'

'Not so fast, children, there's no hurry. Let Mr. Learn-a-lot get nicely into bed first.'

'He's climbing into bed now, Mama! He's in bed, really he is, Mama! Wouldn't it be dreadful if he fell asleep before he heard our singing, Mama?' squeaked all the little midges. But Mrs. Midge was sure the schoolmaster would wake up again when they started singing.

'I think Big Sister Midge had better go in first,' she said.

'All right, but what am I to sing, Mama?'

'You can sing the song about "We midges have not got . . .",' said Mrs. Midge, and settled herself with her two younger daughters behind the curtain. 'And remember to fly in a circle over his head. If he likes your song he will sit up in bed. Now off you go!'

And Big Sister Midge flew round and round in a circle over Mr. Learn-a-lot's head and sang this song:

'We midges have not got a couple of beans
Yet in summer we all are as happy as queens,
For every night in a swoon of delight
We dance to the tune of our dizzy flight,
And all we need to keep in the pink
Is a tiny drop of your blood to drink.'

Three times she sang the same verse, and she was beginning to think Mr. Learn-a-lot didn't care for her song at all. But suddenly he sat bolt upright in bed.

'Come back! Come back, child!' whispered Mrs. Midge.

'Was I all right, Mama?'

'You were very good. Now we'll just wait till Mr. Learn-a-lot has fallen asleep again, then it'll be Middle Sister's turn. You can sing the song about "How doth the little busy me"—that is so very funny! There! Now I think it would be all right for you to start. But you mustn't leave off before Mr. Learn-a-lot has got right out of bed and is standing in the middle of the floor. Fly a little higher than your sister did. Off you go!'

And Middle Sister Midge sang as loudly as she could while she flew round and round the schoolmaster's head:

> 'How doth the little busy me
> Improve each shady hour
> By settling on your nose or knee
> As if upon a flower.'

She hadn't sung more than one verse before Mr. Learn-a-lot threw off the bedclothes and tumbled out of bed.

'Come back, come back!' whispered Mrs. Midge.

'Wasn't I good?' said Middle Sister as she arrived back all out of breath. 'And I wasn't a bit afraid of him!'

'That'll do; we midges are not in the habit of boasting,' said Mrs. Midge. 'Now it's Wee Sister's turn.'

'What shall I sing?' asked the smallest midge with the tiniest voice you ever heard.

'You can sing our evening song—you know—the one that goes:

> 'The day is done and all rejoice
> To hear again this still small voice.
> May the music of my wings
> Console you for my little stings.'

That's just the thing for tonight,' Mrs. Midge added thoughtfully.

'Oh yes, I know that one,' said Wee Sister; she was very pleased her mother had chosen one she knew.

'I expect it will be the last song tonight,' said Mrs. Midge, 'and don't worry if you don't get right through it. If Mr. Learn-a-lot suddenly claps his hands you must be sure to come back to me at once. Will you remember that?'

'Yes, Mama,' said Wee Sister, and off she flew.

Mr. Learn-a-lot was lying absolutely still. So Wee Sister began to sing—all on one top note:

'The day is done——'

Smack! Mr. Learn-a-lot clapped his hands together.

'Come back, come back!' called Mrs. Midge. But there was no sign of Wee Sister.

'Oh, my darling, sweet wee one, please come back to your mother!' wailed Mrs. Midge. No sound—no sound at all for a long time; then suddenly Wee Sister was sitting on the curtain beside them.

'Didn't you hear me calling?' asked Mrs. Midge very sternly.

'Oh yes, but you said I was to fly very, very quietly, and that clap of Mr. Learn-a-lot's sent me flying right into the darkest corner of the room.'

'Poor darling!' said Mrs. Midge. 'But you're safe back now. You've all been very good and very clever girls. And now I'd like to hear what you think of Mr. Learn-a-lot?'

Big Sister answered, 'He's nice; he likes the one who sings longest best!'

Middle Sister answered, 'He's very polite; he gets out of bed for the one who sings loudest!'

And Wee Sister said, 'I think he's very musical; he claps the one with the sweetest voice!'

'Yes, yes, that's all very true,' said Mrs. Midge; 'but now I will tell you something else about Mr. Learn-a-lot. He is not only a very learned gentleman, but he will provide us with the nicest, most enjoyable supper, and we needn't even wake him up. Shall we go?'

'Oh, that is a fine idea!'cried Big Sister, Middle Sister and Wee Sister Midge, for they always did just what their mother told them.

Poor Mr. Learn-a-lot!

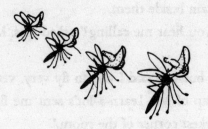

'Oh no, you can't fool me like you did the fox,' said the wolf.

'I'm not trying to fool you at all,' said Mrs Pepperpot; she had a good idea and was no longer afraid. 'You'd better do as I say or I'll send for One-eye Threadless!'

The wolf laughed. 'I've heard many old wives' tales but I've never heard that one before!'

'It's not an old wives' tale,' said Mrs Pepperpot indignantly, 'and I'm not just an old wife; I'm Mrs Pepperpot who can shrink and grow again all in a flash. One-eye Threadless is my servant.'

Alf Prøysen

Mrs PEPPERPOT
AGAIN

Illustrated by Björn Berg

Contents

Mrs. Pepperpot tries to please her husband

THINGS were not very lively at Mrs. Pepperpot's house. Mr. Pepperpot was in a bad mood—he had been in it for days—and Mrs. Pepperpot simply didn't know how to get him out of it. She put flowers on the table and cooked him his favourite dish, fried bacon with macaroni cheese. But it was all no use; Mr. Pepperpot just went on moping.

'I don't know what's the matter with him,' sighed Mrs. Pepperpot, 'perhaps he's pining for pancakes.' So she made him a big pile of pancakes.

When her husband came in for dinner his face lit up at the sight of them, but as soon as he'd sat down and picked up his knife and fork to start eating, his face fell again; he was as glum as before.

'Ah well!' he said, staring up at the ceiling, 'I suppose it's too much to expect.'

'I've had enough of this!' cried Mrs. Pepperpot. 'You tell me what's wrong, or I'll *shrink*, so I will!' (You remember that Mrs. Pepperpot had a habit of shrinking to the size of a pepperpot, though not usually, I'm afraid, when she *wanted* to, but at the most inconvenient moments.) 'You have something on your mind, that's quite clear,' she went on. 'But you don't think of me, do you? Watching your face getting longer every day is no joke, I can tell you. Now even pancakes can't cheer you up.'

'Pancakes are all right,' nodded Mr. Pepperpot, 'but there's something else missing.'

'What could that be?' asked his wife.

'Couldn't we sometimes have a bit of bilberry jam with the pancakes, instead of just eating them plain?' And Mr. Pepperpot gave a great sigh.

At last she understood; it *was* a very long time since she had given him bilberry jam, and that was what the poor man had been missing.

'Well, if that's all you want, I'll go and pick some bilberries this very minute,' said Mrs. Pepperpot, and she snatched a bucket from a hook on the wall and rushed out of the door.

She walked rather fast because she was cross with her husband, and as she walked she talked to herself: 'I've got the silliest husband alive,' she muttered. 'I was a fool to marry him. In fact, there's only one bigger fool than me, and that's him. *Oh*, how stupid he is!'

In no time at all she reached the spot in the forest where the bilberries grew. She put her bucket under a bush and started picking into the cup she had in her apron pocket. Every time the cup was full she emptied it into the bucket. Cup after cup went in, until the bucket needed only one more cup to be quite full. But then, just as she had picked the last bilberry into the cup, lo and behold! She shrank to the size of a pepperpot.

'Now we're in a jam, that's certain, and I don't mean bilberry jam!' said the little old woman, who now had a tiny voice like a mouse. 'Still, I expect I can manage to get the cup as far as the bucket if I push and pull hard enough. After that we'll have to think again.'

So she crooked her arm through the handle and dragged the cup along. It was very hard at first, but then she came to an ant-path made of slippery pine-needles; here it was much easier, because the cup could slide along it. And all the time little ants and big ants kept scuttling to and fro beside her. She tried to talk to them.

'How d'you do, ants,' she said. 'Hard at work, I see. Yes, there's always plenty to do and that's a fact.' But the ants were far too busy to answer.

'Couldn't you stop for a minute and talk to me?' she asked. But they just hurried on. 'Well, I shall have to talk to myself; then I won't be disturbing anybody.' And she sat down with her back leaning against the cup.

As she sat there, she suddenly felt something breathe down her neck; she turned round, and saw a fox standing there waving his tail in a friendly sort of way.

'Hullo, Mr. Fox. Are you out for a stroll?' said Mrs. Pepperpot. 'Lucky you don't know my hens are . . . Oh dear! I nearly let my tongue run away with me!'

'Where did you say your hens were, Mrs. Pepperpot?' asked the fox in his silkiest voice.

'That would be telling, wouldn't it?' said Mrs. Pepperpot. 'But, as you see, I'm rather busy just now; I've got to get this cup of bilberries hauled over to the bucket somehow, so I haven't time to talk to you.'

'I'll carry the cup for you,' said the fox, as polite as could be. 'Then you can talk while we walk.'

'Thanks very much,' said Mrs. Pepperpot. 'As I was saying, my hens are . . . There now! I nearly said it again!'

The fox smiled encouragingly: 'Just go on talking, it doesn't matter what you say to *me*.'

'I'm not usually one to gossip, but somehow it seems so easy to talk about my hens being . . . Goodness, why don't I keep my mouth shut? Anyway, there's the bucket. So, if you would be so kind and set the cup down beside it I'll tell you where my hens are.'

'That's right, you tell me. Your hens will be quite safe with me.'

'They certainly will!' laughed Mrs. Pepperpot, 'for they're all away! They were broody, so I lent them to the neighbours to hatch out their eggs.'

Then the fox saw he had been tricked, and he was so ashamed he slunk away into the forest and hid himself.

'Ha, ha, ha! That was a fine trick you played on the fox!' said a voice quite close to Mrs. Pepperpot. She looked up and there stood a wolf towering over her.

'Well, if it isn't Mr. Wolf!' said Mrs. Pepperpot, swallowing hard to keep up her courage. 'The ve .. very person I need. You can help me tip this cup of bilberries into the bucket.'

'Oh no, you can't fool me like you did the fox,' said the wolf.

'I'm not trying to fool you at all,' said Mrs. Pepperpot; she had had a good idea and was no longer afraid. 'You'd better do as I say or I'll send for One-eye Threadless!'

The wolf laughed. 'I've heard many old wives' tales but I've never heard that one before!'

'It's not an old wives' tale,' said Mrs. Pepperpot indignantly, 'and I'm not just an old wife; I'm Mrs. Pepperpot who can shrink and grow again all in a flash. One-eye Threadless is my servant.'

'Ha, ha! I'd like to see that servant of yours!' laughed the wolf.

'Very well; stick your nose into my apron pocket here and you'll meet him,' said Mrs. Pepperpot. So the wolf put his nose in her apron pocket and pricked it very severely on a needle she kept there.

'Ow, ow!' he shouted and started running towards the forest. But Mrs. Pepperpot called him back at once: 'Come here! You haven't done your job yet; empty that cup into that bucket, and don't you dare spill a single berry, or I'll send for One-eye Threadless to prick you again!'

The wolf didn't dare disobey her, but as soon as he had emptied the cup into the bucket he ran like the fox to the forest to hide.

Mrs. Pepperpot had a good laugh as she watched him go, but then she heard something rustle near the bucket. This time it was the big brown bear himself.

'Dear me! What an honour!' said Mrs. Pepperpot in a shaky voice, and she curtsied so low she nearly disappeared in the bushes. 'Has the fine weather tempted Your Majesty out for a walk?'

'Yes,' growled the big brown bear and went on sniffing at the bucket.

'How very fortunate for me! As Your Majesty can see, I've picked a whole bucket of berries, but it's not very safe for a little old woman like myself to walk in the forest alone. Could I ask Your Majesty to carry the bucket out to the road for me?'

'I don't know about that,' said the bear. 'I like bilberries myself.'

'Yes, of course, but you're not like the rest of them,

Your Majesty; you wouldn't rob a poor little old woman like me!'

'Bilberries; that's what I want!' said the bear, and put his head down to start eating.

In a flash Mrs. Pepperpot had jumped on his neck and started tickling him behind his ears.

'What are you doing?' asked the bear.

'I'm just tickling your ears for you,' answered Mrs. Pepperpot. 'Doesn't it feel good?'

'Good? It's almost better than eating the berries!' said the bear.

'Well, if Your Majesty would be so kind as to carry the bucket, I could be tickling Your Majesty's ears all the way,' said the artful Mrs. Pepperpot.

'Oh, very well then,' grumbled the bear.

When they reached the road the bear put the bucket down very carefully on a flat stone.

'Many, many thanks, Your Majesty,' said Mrs. Pepperpot as she made another deep curtsey.

'Thank *you*,' said the bear, and shuffled off into the forest.

When the bear had gone Mrs. Pepperpot became her usual size again, so she picked up her bucket and hurried homeward.

'It's really not very difficult to look after yourself, even when you're only the size of a pepperpot,' she told herself. 'As long as you know how to tackle the people you meet. Cunning people must be tricked, cowardly ones must be frightened, and the big, strong ones must have their ears tickled.'

As for bad-tempered husbands, the only thing to do with *them* is to give them bilberry jam with their pancakes.

Mrs. Pepperpot minds the baby

Now I'll tell you what happened the day Mrs. Pepperpot was asked to mind the baby.

It was early in the morning. Mrs. Pepperpot had sent her husband off to work. In the usual way wives do, she had made the coffee and the sandwiches for his lunch, and had stood by the window and waved till he was out of sight. Then, just like other wives, she had gone back to bed to have a little extra shut-eye, leaving all her housework for later.

She had been sleeping a couple of hours when there was a knock at the door. She looked at the clock. 'Good heavens!' she cried, 'have I slept so long?' She pulled her clothes on very quickly and ran to open the door.

In the porch stood a lady with a little boy on her arm.

'Forgive me for knocking,' said the lady.

'You're welcome,' said Mrs. Pepperpot.

'You see,' said the lady, 'I'm staying with my aunt near here with my little boy, and today we simply *have* to go shopping in the town. I can't take Roger and there's no one in the house to look after him.'

'Oh, that's all right!' said Mrs. Pepperpot. 'I'll look after your little boy.' (To herself she thought: 'However will I manage with all that work and me oversleeping like that. Ah well, I shall have to do both at the same time.') Then she said out loud: 'Roger, come to Mrs. Pepperpot? That's right!' And she took the baby from the lady.

'You don't need to give him a meal,' said the lady. 'I've brought some apples he can have when he starts sucking his fingers.'

'Very well,' said Mrs. Pepperpot, and put the apples in a dish on the sideboard.

The lady said goodbye and Mrs. Pepperpot set the baby down on the rug in the sitting-room. Then she went out into the kitchen to fetch her broom to start sweeping up. At that very moment she *shrank*!

'Oh dear! Oh dear! Whatever shall I do?' she wailed, for of course now she was much smaller than the baby. She gave up any idea of cleaning the house; when her husband came home she would have to tell him that she had had a headache.

'I must go and see what that little fellow is doing,' she thought, as she climbed over the doorstep into the sitting-room. Not a moment too soon! For Roger had crawled right across the floor and was just about to pull the tablecloth off the table together with a pot of jam, a loaf of bread, and a big jug of coffee.

Mrs. Pepperpot lost no time. She knew it was too far for her to get to the table, so she pushed over a large silver cup which was standing on the floor, waiting to be polished. Her husband had won it in a skiing competition years ago when he was young.

The cup made a fine booming noise as it fell; the baby turned round and started crawling towards it.

'That's right,' said Mrs. Pepperpot, 'you play with that; at least you can't break it.'

But Roger wasn't after the silver cup. Gurgling: 'Ha' dolly! Ha' dolly!' he made a bee-line for Mrs. Pepperpot, and before she could get away, he had grabbed her by the waist! He jogged her up and down and every time Mrs. Pepperpot kicked and wriggled to get free, he laughed. ''Ickle, 'ickle!' he shouted, for she was tickling his hand with her feet.

'Let go! Let go!' yelled Mrs. Pepperpot. But Roger was used to his father shouting 'Let's go!' when he threw him up in the air and caught him again. So Roger shouted 'Leggo! Leggo!' and threw the little old woman up in the air with all the strength of his short arms. Mrs. Pepperpot went up and up—nearly to the ceiling! Luckily she landed on the sofa, but she bounced several times before she could stop.

'Talk of flying through the air with the greatest of ease!' she gasped. 'If that had happened to me in my normal size I'd most likely have broken every bone in my body. Ah well, I'd better see what my little friend is up to now.'

She soon found out. Roger had got hold of a match-box and was trying to strike a match. Luckily he was using the wrong side of the box, but Mrs. Pepperpot had to think very quickly indeed.

'Youngsters like to copy everything you do, so I'll take this nut and throw it at him. Then he'll throw it at me—I hope.'

She had found the nut in the sofa and now she was in such a hurry to throw it she forgot to aim properly. But it was a lucky shot and it hit Roger just behind the ear, making him turn round. 'What else can I throw?' wondered Mrs. Pepperpot, but there was no need, because the baby had seen her; he dropped the match-box and started crawling towards the sofa.

'Ha' dolly! Ha' dolly!' he gurgled delightedly. And now they started a very funny game of hide-and-seek— at least it was fun for Roger, but not quite so amusing for poor little old Mrs. Pepperpot who had to hide behind the cushions to get away from him. In the end she managed to climb on to the sideboard where she kept a precious geranium in a pot.

'Aha, you can't catch me now!' she said, feeling much safer.

But at that moment the baby decided to go back to the match-box. 'No, no, no!' shouted Mrs. Pepperpot. Roger took no notice. So, when she saw he was trying to strike another match, she put her back against the flowerpot and gave it a push so that it fell to the floor with a crash.

Roger immediately left the match-box for this new and interesting mess of earth and bits of broken flowerpot. He buried both his hands in it and started putting it in his mouth, gurgling, 'Nice din-din!'

'No, no, no!' shouted Mrs. Pepperpot once more. 'Oh, whatever shall I do?' Her eye caught the apples left by Roger's mother. They were right beside her on the dish. One after the other she rolled them over the edge of the dish on to the floor. Roger watched them roll, then he decided to chase them, forgetting his lovely meal of earth and broken flowerpot. Soon the apples were all over the floor and the baby was crawling happily from one to the other.

There was a knock on the door.

'Come in,' said Mrs. Pepperpot.

Roger's mother opened the door and came in, and there was Mrs. Pepperpot as large as life, carrying a dust-pan full of earth and broken bits in one hand and her broom in the other.

'Has he been naughty?' asked the lady.

'As good as gold,' said Mrs. Pepperpot. 'We've had a high old time together, haven't we, Roger?' And she handed him back to his mother.

'I'll have to take you home now, precious,' said the lady.

But the little fellow began to cry. 'Ha' dolly! Ha' dolly!' he sobbed.

'Have *dolly*?' said his mother. 'But you didn't bring a dolly—you don't even have one at home.' She turned to Mrs. Pepperpot. 'I don't know what he means.'

'Oh, children say so many things grown-ups don't understand,' said Mrs. Pepperpot, and waved goodbye to Roger and his mother.

Then she set about cleaning up her house.

Mrs. Pepperpot's penny watchman

STRANGE things had been happening in Mrs. Pepperpot's house. It all began when a little girl came to the door selling penny raffle tickets for a tablecloth. Mrs. Pepperpot hunted high and low until she found a penny; it was a nice shiny one, because someone had been polishing it. But just as she was writing her name on the ticket, the penny dropped on the floor and rolled into a crack by the trapdoor to the cellar.

'Bang goes my fortune,' said Mrs. Pepperpot, as she watched it disappear. 'Now I won't be able to buy a raffle ticket after all. But I can't let you go without giving you anything; what about a nice home-made short-cake?' And she stood on a stool to reach the cake-tin.

It was empty. Mrs. Pepperpot turned the tin almost inside out, but there was no sign of any short-cake.

'I can't understand it,' she said. 'I baked two whole rounds of short-cake on Friday. Today it's only Monday, and the tin is empty. Very mysterious. But I've got something you might like even better, little girl.' So

24

saying, Mrs. Pepperpot opened the trapdoor to the cellar
and went down the steps to fetch the big jar of bramble
jelly she had left over from the summer.

But what a sight met her eyes!

'Goodness Gracious and Glory Be!' she exclaimed,
for the big jar of bramble jelly was lying smashed under
the shelf with the jelly gently oozing out over the floor.
From the sticky mess a little trail of mouse footprints
ran across to the chimney.

There was nothing for it—Mrs. Pepperpot had to go
up to the little girl and tell her she couldn't even have
bramble jelly. But the little girl said it didn't matter a bit
and politely curtsied before going on to the next house.

Mrs. Pepperpot took a mouse-trap and went down the cellar steps again. She baited it with cheese and set it very carefully on the floor. When it was done she turned to go upstairs again, but the hem of her skirt brushed against it, and SNAP! went the trap, with a corner of her skirt caught in it. That was bad enough, but then, if you please, she shrank again!

'Now I really *am* stuck!' she told herself, and she certainly was; she couldn't move an inch. After she had sat there a while she saw a young mouse peeping over the edge of an empty flowerpot.

'You're quite safe to come out,' said Mrs. Pepperpot. 'I'm too well tethered to do you any harm at the moment.'

But the little mouse darted off to an empty cardboard box and then two little mice popped their noses over the edge.

'One and one makes two,' said Mrs. Pepperpot. 'I learned that at school, and I wouldn't be a bit surprised if you fetched a third one—for one and two make three!'

She was right. The two little mice darted off together and stayed away quite a long time while she sat and waited. Suddenly she heard a tinny little sound. Ping! Ping! And a big mouse came walking towards her on his hind legs, banging a shiny gong with a little steel pin. The shiny gong was Mrs. Pepperpot's lost penny!

The big mouse bowed low. 'Queen of the House, I greet you!' The little mice were peeping out from behind him.

'Thank goodness for that!' said Mrs. Pepperpot. 'For a moment I thought you might be coming to gobble me up—you're so much bigger than I am!'

'We're not in the habit of gobbling up queens,' said the large mouse. 'I just wanted to tell you, you have a thief in your house.'

Mrs. Pepperpot snorted. 'Thief indeed! Of course I have; you and all the other mice are the thieves in my house. Whose penny is it you're using for a gong, may I ask?'

'Oh, is that what it is? A penny?' said the big mouse. 'Well, it rolled through a crack in the floor, you see, so I thought I could use it to scare away the thief and to show I'm the watchman in this house. You really do need a watchman, Queen of the House, to keep an eye on things for you.'

'What nonsense!' said Mrs. Pepperpot. She tried to stand up, but it was rather difficult with her dress caught in the trap and she herself so tiny.

'Take it easy, Queen of the House,' said the big mouse. 'Let my son here tell you what he has seen.'

Timidly, one of the little mice came forward and told how he had climbed up the chimney one day and peeped through a hole into the kitchen. There he had seen a terrible monster who was eating up all the cake in the tin.

Then the other little mouse chirped in to tell how he had been playing hide-and-seek behind a jam-jar on the shelf when the monster had put out a huge hand and taken the jar away. But he had been so scared when he saw the little mouse that he had dropped the jar on the floor, and all the bramble jelly came pouring out.

Suddenly they heard Tramp! Tramp! Tramp! up above; the sound of huge boots walking about.

'That's the monster!' said one of the little mice.

'Yes, that's him all right!' said the other little mouse.

'Is it, indeed!' said Mrs. Pepperpot. 'If only I could get out of this trap, I should very much like to go and have a look at this monster.'

'We'll help you,' said all the mice, and they set to work to free Mrs. Pepperpot from the trap in the way only mice know how; they gnawed through her skirt, leaving a piece stuck in the spring.

'Now you must hurry up to the kitchen to see the monster,' they said.

'But how am I to get there?' asked Mrs. Pepperpot.

'Up through the chimney on our special rope; we'll pull you up.'

And that's what they did. They hoisted Mrs. Pepperpot higher and higher inside the chimney, until she could see a chink of light.

'That's the crack into the kitchen,' the big mouse told her from below.

She called down to him: 'Thank you Mr. Watchman, thank you for your help, and keep a sharp look-out!'

Then she climbed through the hole in the wall. As soon as she set foot on the floor she grew to her normal size. Standing in front of the stove, she put her hands on her hips and said, 'So it's you, husband, is it, who's been eating all my short-cake and stealing the bramble jelly in the cellar?'

Mr. Pepperpot looked dumbfounded: 'How did you know that?' he said.

'Because I have a watchman now, I have paid him a penny,' said Mrs. Pepperpot.

The bad luck story

IF YOU take the road past Mrs. Pepperpot's house and turn to the right, then to the left and carry straight on, you will come to a cottage.

In this cottage lived an old woman they called 'Mrs. Calamity', because she believed in omens and always expected the worst to happen. Another curious thing about her was that she had the habit of stealing cuttings from pot-plants in other people's houses. Not that this in itself was very serious, only sometimes the flowers died after she had been cutting them about. But Mrs. Calamity had the idea that stolen plants thrive much better than any you got as a present, which is just one of those old wives' tales.

One day she visited little old Mrs. Pepperpot. She sat on the edge of a chair very politely and talked about this and that, but all the time she was looking round at all the plants in Mrs. Pepperpot's window-sill.

'That's right; have a good look,' thought Mrs. Pepperpot to herself. 'I know what you're after; you want to take cuttings of my best geranium. But we'll see about that, my fine lady!'

Unfortunately, there was a knock at the door just at that moment, and Mrs. Pepperpot had to leave her visitor alone while she went to answer it.

A man stood there. 'Anyone called Cuthbertson live here?' he asked.

'Cuthbertson? There's never been anyone of that name in this house, as far as I know,' said Mrs. Pepperpot. 'You'd better ask at the post-office. Excuse me, I'm busy just now.' And she turned to shut the door.

Too late! For at that moment Mrs. Pepperpot shrank again!

She stretched her little neck as much as she could to look over the doorstep into the sitting-room. Sure enough! There was Mrs. Calamity ferreting about in Mrs. Pepperpot's flowerpots.

'I have a feeling you're going to regret that, Madam Thief,' thought Mrs. Pepperpot as she swung herself over the step into the yard. There she found a little wagtail pecking about, looking for something to eat.

'Hullo, little wagtail,' she said. 'If you'll help *me*, then I'll help *you*. You can have all the crumbs you want if you'll just go over to the front doorstep and stand quite still, facing the door.'

'That's easily done,' said the wagtail, and hopped across the yard.

No doubt Mrs. Calamity was wondering what had happened to the lady of the house. She came to the door and looked out, holding her hand carefully over her apron pocket where she had hidden the geranium cutting.

Then she caught sight of the wagtail on the step. 'Oh Calamity!' she wailed. 'I've looked a wagtail straight in the face and now I shall have bad luck for a year.'

And, clutching her apron pocket, she hurried away from the house.

But over her head the wagtail was following her, flying with Mrs. Pepperpot on its back. As she clung with her arms round the bird's neck, she said: 'D'you know where we could find a black cat?'

'A black cat?' answered the wagtail. 'I should think I do! The horrible creature was lying in wait for me down by the bend in the road. She's probably still there. So don't ask me to land anywhere near her.'

'Don't worry!' said Mrs. Pepperpot. 'I want you to put me down on the *opposite* side of the road—I have a little plan.'

So the wagtail did as she asked and flew out of harm's way as fast as it could go.

Mrs. Pepperpot crouched down in the long grass; she could see the cat's tail waving to and fro in the ditch

on the other side of the road. Soon she heard the clump, clump, clump of Mrs. Calamity's boots as she walked down the road.

Just as she came past where Mrs. Pepperpot was

hiding, Mrs. Pepperpot made the noise of a wagtail calling. The black cat heard it and, like a streak of lightning, shot across the road, right in front of Mrs. Calamity.

Mrs. Calamity stood stock-still with fright. 'A black cat!' she screamed. 'That means *three* years' bad luck!

Oh Calamity, what shall I do?' She was so alarmed she didn't dare go on; instead, she took the path through the wood to her house.

Meanwhile the cat was going in the same direction, for by now Mrs. Pepperpot was riding on her back. 'Have you seen any magpies about?' she asked the cat.

'I should think I have!' said the cat. 'There's a pair of them in that birch-tree over there; they tease me and pull my tail whenever they get the chance. Look! They're waiting for me now!'

'Then you can drop me here,' said Mrs. Pepperpot. 'Come and see me tomorrow and I'll give you a bowl of cream.'

The cat did as she asked, and a moment later Mrs. Pepperpot was talking to the magpies in the birch-tree.

'Good afternoon,' she said. 'I wonder if you would have such a thing as a key-ring in your nest?'

'Oh no,' said the magpies, 'we don't have key-rings, we only collect broken-mirror bits.'

'The best is good enough,' replied Mrs. Pepperpot. 'I want you to put some nice-looking bits on Mrs. Calamity's doorstep. If you can do that for me, I'll keep the curly tail for you when we kill the pig at Christmas.'

The magpies didn't need to be told twice. A little heap of broken-mirror bits were on Mrs. Calamity's doorstep before you could say Jack Robinson.

When she arrived and saw what was waiting for her Mrs. Calamity sat down and cried.

'Oh, misery me! Oh Calamity! A broken mirror will give me *seven* years' bad luck!'

But by now Mrs. Pepperpot had grown to her proper size again; quietly she came round the corner, and her voice was quite gentle when she spoke.

'Now, now, Mrs. Calamity,' she said, 'you mustn't sit here crying.'

'Oh, Mrs. Pepperpot! It's nothing but bad luck for me from beginning to end.' She sniffed, and she told Mrs. Pepperpot about the wagtail that had faced her, the cat that had jumped across her path and now the broken mirror. When she'd finished she fished for a handkerchief in her apron pocket.

Out fell the geranium cutting!

Mrs. Calamity picked it up and handed it to Mrs. Pepperpot. 'There—take it! I stole it from your house. Now you'd better have it back, for I shall never need geraniums or anything else in this world, I don't suppose!'

'Don't be silly,' said Mrs. Pepperpot. 'Let's forget about all this nonsense, shall we? I'm going to *give* you the cutting as a present. You plant it, and I'm sure you'll find that it'll grow into the finest flower you ever had.'

She was right. The tiny cutting grew into a huge geranium with bright red blooms, and that in spite of the fact that Mrs. Calamity not only thanked Mrs. Pepperpot, but shook hands as well, which is the worst thing you can do if you believe in bad omens.

But from then on she changed her ideas, and people no longer called her Mrs. Calamity, but plain Mrs. Brown instead.

Mrs. Pepperpot and the moose

IT WAS winter-time, and Mrs. Pepperpot was having trouble getting water. The tap in her kitchen ran slower and slower, until one day it just dripped and then stopped altogether. The well was empty.

'Ah, well,' thought Mrs. Pepperpot, 'it won't be the first time I've had this kind of trouble, and it won't be the last. But with two strong arms and a good sound bucket, not to mention the lucky chance that there's another well down by the forest fence, we'll soon fix that.'

So she put on her husband's old winter coat and a pair of thick gloves and fetched a pick-axe from the wood-shed. Then she trudged through the snow down the hill, to where there was a dip by the forest fence. She swept the snow away and started breaking a hole in the ice with the pick-axe. Chips of ice flew everywhere as Mrs. Pepperpot hacked away, not looking to left or right. She made such a noise that she never heard the sound of breaking twigs, nor the snorting that was coming from the other side of the fence.

But there he was; a huge moose with great big antlers, not moving at all, but staring angrily at Mrs. Pepperpot. Suddenly he gave a very loud snort and leaped over the fence, butting Mrs. Pepperpot from behind, so that she went head-first into a pile of snow!

'What the dickens!' cried Mrs. Pepperpot as she scrambled to her feet. But by that time the moose was back on the other side of the fence. When she saw what

it was that had pushed her over, Mrs. Pepperpot lost no time in scrambling up the hill and into her house, locking the door behind her. Then she peeped out of the kitchen window to see if the moose was still there. He was.

'You wait, you great big brute!' said Mrs. Pepperpot. 'I'll give you a fright you won't forget!'

She put on a black rain-cape and a battered old hat, and in her hand she carried a big stick. Then she crept out of the door and hid round the corner of the house.

The moose was quietly nibbling the bark off the trees and seemed to be taking no notice of her.

Suddenly she stormed down the hill, shouting, 'Woollah, Woollah, Woollah!' like a Red Indian, the black rain-cape flapping round her and the stick waving in the air. The moose *should* have been frightened, but he just took one look at the whirling thing coming towards him, leaped the fence and headed straight for it!

Poor Mrs. Pepperpot! All she could do was to rush back indoors again as fast as she knew how.

'Now what shall I do?' she wondered. 'I must have water to cook my potatoes and do my washing-up, and a little cup of coffee wouldn't come amiss after all this excitement. Perhaps if I were to put on my old man's trousers and take his gun out . . . I could pretend to aim it; that might scare him off.'

So she put on the trousers and took out the gun; but this was the silliest idea she had had yet, because, before she was half-way down the hill, that moose came pounding towards her on his great long legs. She never had time to point the gun. Worse still, she dropped it in her efforts to keep the trousers up and run back to the house at the same time. When the moose saw her disappear indoors, he turned and stalked down the hill again, but this time he didn't jump back over the fence, but stayed by the well, as if he were guarding it.

'Ah well,' said Mrs. Pepperpot, 'I suppose I shall have to fill the bucket with snow and melt it to get the water I need. That moose is clearly not afraid of anything.'

So she took her bucket and went outside. But just as she was bending down to scoop up the snow, she turned small! But this time the magic worked quicker than usual, and somehow she managed to tumble into the bucket which was lying on its side. The bucket started to roll down the hill; faster and faster it went, and poor Mrs. Pepperpot was seeing stars as she bumped round and round inside.

Just above the dip near the well a little mound jutted out, and here the bucket made a leap into space. 'This is the end of me!' thought Mrs. Pepperpot. She waited for the bump, but it didn't come! Instead the bucket seemed to be floating through the air, over the

fence and right into the forest. If she had had time to
think, Mrs. Pepperpot would have known that the
moose had somehow caught the bucket on one of his
antlers, but it is not so easy to think when you're swinging between heaven and earth.

At last the bucket got stuck on a branch and the
moose thundered on through the undergrowth. Mrs.
Pepperpot lay there panting, trying to get her breath
back. She had no idea where she was. But then she heard:
'Chuck, chuck! Chuck, chuck!'—the chattering of a
squirrel as he ran down the tree-trunk over her head.

'Hullo!' said the squirrel, 'if it isn't Mrs. Pepperpot!
Out for a walk, or something?'

'Not exactly a *walk*,' said Mrs. Pepperpot, 'but I've had a free ride, though I don't know who gave it to me.'

'That was the King of the Moose,' said the squirrel. 'I saw him gallop past with a wild look in his eyes. It's the first time I have ever seen him afraid, I can tell you that. He is so stupid and so stuck-up you wouldn't believe it. All he thinks of is fighting; he goes for anything and anybody—the bigger the better. But you seem to have given him the fright of his life.'

'I'm glad I managed it in the end,' said Mrs. Pepperpot, 'and now I'd be gladder still if I knew how to get myself home.'

But she needn't have worried, because at that moment she felt herself grow large again, and the next thing she knew she had broken the branch and was lying on the ground. She picked herself and her bucket up and started walking home. But when she got to the fence she took a turn down to the well to fill the bucket.

When she stood up she looked back towards the forest, and there, sure enough, stood the moose, blinking at her. But Mrs. Pepperpot was no longer afraid of him. All she had to do was to rattle that bucket a little, and the big creature shook his head and disappeared silently into the forest.

From that day on Mrs. Pepperpot had no trouble fetching water from the well by the forest fence.

Mrs. Pepperpot finds a hidden treasure

IT WAS a fine sunny day in January, and Mrs. Pepperpot was peeling potatoes at the kitchen sink.

'Miaow!' said the cat; she was lying in front of the stove.

'Miaow yourself!' answered Mrs. Pepperpot.

'Miaow!' said the cat again.

Mrs. Pepperpot suddenly remembered an old, old rhyme she learned when she was a child. It went like this:

The cat sat by the fire,
Her aches and pains were dire,
Such throbbing in my head,
She cried; I'll soon be dead!

'Poor Pussy! Are your aches and pains so bad? Does your head throb?' she said, and smiled down at the cat.

But the cat only looked at her.

Mrs. Pepperpot stopped peeling potatoes, wiped her hands and knelt down beside the cat. 'There's something you want to tell me, isn't there, Pussy? It's too bad I can't understand you except when I'm little, but it's not my fault.' She stroked the cat, but Pussy didn't purr, just went on looking at her.

'Well, I can't spend all day being sorry for you, my girl, I've got a husband to feed,' said Mrs. Pepperpot, and went back to the potatoes in the sink. When they were ready she put them in a saucepan of cold water on the stove, not forgetting a good pinch of salt. After that she laid the table, for her husband had to have his dinner sharp at one o'clock and it was now half past twelve.

Pussy was at the door now. 'Miaow!' she said, scratching at it.

'You want to get out, do you?' said Mrs. Pepperpot, and opened the door. She followed the cat out, because she had noticed that her broom had fallen over in the snow. The door closed behind her.

And at that moment she shrank to her pepperpot size!

'About time too!' said the cat. 'I've been waiting for days for this to happen. Now don't let's waste any more time; jump on my back! We're setting off at once.'

Mrs. Pepperpot didn't stop to ask where they were going; she climbed on Pussy's back. 'Hold on tight!' said Pussy, and bounded off down the little bank at the back of the house past Mrs. Pepperpot's rubbish-heap.

'We're coming to the first hindrance,' said Pussy; 'just sit tight and don't say a word!' All Mrs. Pepperpot could see was a single birch-tree with a couple of magpies on it. True, the birds seemed as big as eagles to her now and the tree was like a mountain. But when the magpies started screeching she knew what the cat meant.

'There's the cat! There's the cat!' they screamed. 'Let's nip her tail! Let's pull her whiskers!' And they swooped down, skimming so close over Mrs. Pepperpot's head she was nearly blown off the cat's back. But the cat took no notice at all, just kept steadily on down the hill, and the magpies soon tired of the game.

'That's that!' said the cat. 'The next thing we have to watch out for is being hit by snowballs. We have to cross the boys' playground now, so if any of them start aiming at you, duck behind my ears and hang on!'

Mrs. Pepperpot looked at the boys; she knew them all, she had often given them sweets and biscuits. '*They* can't be dangerous,' she said to herself.

But then she heard one of them say: 'There comes that stupid cat; let's see who can hit it first! Come on,

boys!' And they all started pelting snowballs as hard as they could.

Suddenly remembering how small she was, Mrs. Pepperpot did as the cat had told her and crouched down behind Pussy's ears until they were safely out of range.

The cat ran on till they got to a wire fence with a hole just big enough for her to wriggle through.

'So far, so good,' she said, 'but now comes the worst bit, because this is dog land, and we don't want to get caught. So keep your eyes skinned!'

The fence divided Mrs. Pepperpot's land from her neighbour's, but she knew the neighbour's dog quite well; he had had many a bone and scraps from her and he was always very friendly. 'We'll be all right here,' she thought.

But she was wrong. Without any warning, that dog suddenly came bearing down on them in great leaps and bounds! Mrs. Pepperpot shook like a jelly when she saw his wide-open jaws all red, with sharp, white teeth glistening in a terrifying way. She flattened herself on the cat's back and clung on for dear life, for Pussy shot like a Sputnik across the yard and straight under the neighbour's barn.

'Phew!' said the cat, 'that was a narrow squeak! Thanks very much for coming all this way with me; I'm afraid it wasn't a very comfortable journey.'

'That's all right,' said Mrs. Pepperpot, 'but perhaps you'll tell me now what we've come for?'

'It's a surprise,' said Pussy, 'but don't worry, you'll get your reward. All we have to do now is to find the hidden treasure, but that means crawling through the hay. So hang on!'

And off they went again, slowly this time, for it was difficult to make their way through the prickly stalks that seemed as big as bean-poles to Mrs. Pepperpot. The dust was terrible; it went in her eyes, her mouth, her hair, down her neck—everywhere.

'Can you see anything?' asked the cat.

'Only blackness,' answered Mrs. Pepperpot, 'and it seems to be getting blacker.'

'In that case we're probably going the right way,' said Pussy, crawling further into the hay. 'D'you see anything now?' she asked.

'Nothing at all,' said Mrs. Pepperpot, for by now her eyes were completely bunged up with hay-seed and dust.

'Try rubbing your eyes,' said the cat, 'for this is where your hidden treasure is.'

So Mrs. Pepperpot rubbed her eyes, blinked and rubbed again until at last she could open them properly. When she did, she was astonished; all round her shone the most wonderful jewels! Diamonds, sapphires, emeralds—they glittered in every hue!

'There you are! Didn't I tell you I had a hidden treasure for you?' said the cat, but she didn't give Mrs. Pepperpot time to have a closer look. 'We'll have to hurry back now, it's nearly time for your husband's dinner.'

So they crawled back through the hay and, just as they got out in the daylight, Mrs. Pepperpot grew to her ordinary size. She picked the cat up in her arms and walked across the yard with her. The dog was there, but what a different dog! He nuzzled Mrs. Pepperpot's skirt and wagged his tail in the friendliest way.

Through the gate they came to the place where the boys were playing. Everyone of them nodded to her and politely said 'Good morning'. Then they went on up the hill, and there were the magpies in the birch-tree. But not a sound came from them; they didn't even seem to notice them walking by.

When they got to the house Mrs. Pepperpot put the cat down and hurried indoors. It was almost one o'clock. She snatched the saucepan from the stove—a few potatoes had stuck to the bottom, so she threw those

out and emptied the rest into a blue serving-bowl. The
saucepan she put outside the back door with cold water
in it.

She had only just got everything ready when Mr.
Pepperpot came in. He sniffed suspiciously. 'I can smell
burnt potatoes,' he said.

'Nonsense,' said Mrs. Pepperpot, 'I dropped a bit of
potato-skin on the stove, that's all. But I've aired the
room since, so just you sit down and eat your dinner.'

'Aren't you having any?' asked her husband.

'Not just now,' answered Mrs. Pepperpot, 'I have to go
and fetch something first. I won't be long.' And Mrs.
Pepperpot went back down the hill, through the gate to
her neighbour's yard, and into the barn. But this time
she climbed *over* the hay till she found the spot where her
hidden treasure lay.

And what d'you think it was?

Four coal-black kittens with shining eyes!

Mr. Pepperpot

Now you have heard a lot about *Mrs.* Pepperpot, but hardly anything about *Mr.* Pepperpot.

He usually comes in at the end of the stories, when Mrs. Pepperpot is back to her normal size and busy with his dinner. If the food isn't ready he always says 'Can't a man ever get his dinner at the proper time in this house?' And if it is ready, he just sits down to eat and says nothing at all. If it's cold out, he says 'Brrrrrrr!' and if it's very hot, he says 'Pheeew!' If Mrs. Pepperpot has done something he doesn't like, he says 'Hmmmmm!' in a disapproving tone of voice. But if he himself is thinking of doing something he doesn't want Mrs. Pepperpot to know about, he goes round the house whistling to himself and humming a little tune.

One evening when he came home, he went up to the attic. Now, Mrs. Pepperpot had hidden four black kittens up there, because Mr. Pepperpot didn't like kittens when they were small (some people don't, you know). So, when Mr. Pepperpot came down from the attic, he stood in the middle of the floor and said 'Hmmmm!' And a little while later he started whistling and humming his tune.

Mrs. Pepperpot said nothing, though she knew what it meant. She just took his old winter coat from its peg and started mending a tear in it.

'What are you mending that for?' asked Mr. Pepperpot.

'The weather's getting so bad, you'll need it,' said Mrs. Pepperpot.

'Who said I was going out?' asked Mr. Pepperpot.

'You can do as you like,' said his wife, 'I'm staying right where I am.'

'Well, maybe I *will* take a turn outside, all the same,' said Mr. Pepperpot.

'I thought you would,' she said.

Mr. Pepperpot went back to the attic, found a big sack and popped the four kittens inside. But when he got to the bottom of the stairs, he thought he would put on the old winter coat. So he put the sack down and went into the kitchen. There he found the coat hanging over a chair.

'I'm going out now!' he called, thinking his wife must be in the sitting-room. He got no answer, but he didn't bother to call again, as he was afraid the kittens might get out of the sack which wasn't properly tied. Quickly he slung it over his shoulder and went out.

It was a nasty night; the wind blew sleet in his face and the road was full of icy puddles.

'Ugh!' said Mr. Pepperpot, 'this weather's fit to drown in!'

'Isn't that just what you're going to do to us poor kittens?' said a tiny voice close by.

Mr. Pepperpot was startled. 'Who said that, I wonder?' he said. He put the sack down to look inside, but as soon as he opened it out jumped one of the kittens and ran off in the darkness.

'Oh dear, what shall I do?' he said, tying up the sack again as quickly as he could. 'I can't leave a kitten running about on a night like this.'

'He won't get any wetter than the rest of us by the time you've finished with us,' said the little voice again.

Mr. Pepperpot untied the sack once more to find out who was speaking. Out jumped the second kitten and disappeared in the sleet and snow. While he hurriedly tied a knot to stop the rest from getting out, he said to himself:

'What if the fox got those two little mites? That would be terrible!'

'No worse than being in *your* hands,' said the tiny voice.

This time, Mr. Pepperpot was very careful to hold his hand over the opening as he untied it. But his foot slipped on the ice and jogged the sack out of his hand, and another kitten got away.

'Three gone! That's bad!' he said.

'Not as bad as it'll be for me!' came the voice from the sack.

'I know who it is now,' said Mr. Pepperpot; 'it's my

old woman who's shrunk again. You're in that sack, aren't you? But I'll catch you! You just wait!' And with that he opened the sack again.

Out jumped the fourth kitten and ran off, lickety-split!

'You can run, I don't care!' said the old man. 'I'm going to catch that wife of mine—it's all her fault!' He got down on his knees and rummaged round in every corner of the sack. But he found nothing—it was quite empty.

Now he really was worried; he was so worried he started sobbing and crying, and in between he called 'Puss, Puss!' and searched all over the place.

A little girl came along the road. 'What have you lost?' she asked.

'Some kittens,' sniffed Mr. Pepperpot.

'I'll help you find them,' said the little girl.

Soon they were joined by a little boy, and he had a torch which made it easier to search. First the little girl found one kitten behind a tree-stump, then the boy found two kittens stuck in a snow-drift, and Mr. Pepperpot himself found the fourth one and put them all back in the sack, tying it very securely this time.

'Thank you for your help,' he said to the children and asked them to take the kittens back to his house and put them in the kitchen.

When they had gone, he started looking for his little old woman. He searched for an hour—for two hours; he called, he begged, he sobbed, he was quite beside himself. But in the end he had to give up. 'I'll go home now,' he said to himself, 'and try again tomorrow.'

But when he got home, there was Mrs. Pepperpot, as large as life, bustling round the kitchen, frying a huge pile of pancakes! And by the kitchen stove was a wicker basket with the mother cat and all four kittens in it.

'When did you come home?' asked the astonished Mr. Pepperpot.

'When did I come home? Why, I've been here all the time, of course,' she said.

'But who was it talking to me from the sack, then?'

'I've no idea,' said Mrs. Pepperpot, 'unless it was your conscience.' And she came over and gave him a great big hug and kiss.

Then Mr. Pepperpot sat down to eat the biggest pile of pancakes he had ever had and all with bilberry jam, and when he was full the kittens finished off the last four.

And after that Mr. and Mrs. Pepperpot lived happily together, and Mrs. Pepperpot gave up shrinking for a very long time indeed—that's why the next story is a made-up story about an OGRE and not about Mrs. Pepperpot at all, at all.

The ogres

IT IS time we made up a story about *ogres*. You see we have to make it up, because there aren't any ogres, really.

First we must have an ogre and he must have a name. Let's call him GAPY GOB, because he's very fond of eating and is always opening his mouth for more.

Good. Gapy Gob has two servants, a little girl and a little boy. The little girl spends all *her* time cooking porridge for her master, so we can call her KATIE COOK. The little boy spends all *his* time chopping wood to burn in the stove on which Katie cooks the porridge. So we can call him CHARLIE CHOP.

Katie Cook and Charlie Chop aren't really ogres at all; they're just ordinary children, but they have no home of their own, so Gapy Gob lets them stay with him. They are very happy there, except for one thing; on the other side of the hill lives an ogress by the name of WILY WINNIE and her servant, a very cunning cat called RIBBY RATSOUP.

Now I think we have enough ogres and people to start the story, don't you?

Wily Winnie was very set on marrying Gapy Gob, because she knew he had a large ham hanging in his larder. Not only that, but Gapy Gob had a much better house than her own and she wanted to live in it. But first she had to get rid of the ogre's two servants, Katie Cook and Charlie Chop.

Several times she had tried to persuade him to send them away, but each time the children had told Gapy Gob that Wily Winnie was just after his ham and that her cat was waiting to eat up all the herrings they had salted down.

One morning early, when Gapy Gob was sitting at the table waiting for Katie to finish stirring his porridge, and

Charlie was sharpening his axe ready for the day's work, there was a knock at the door.

'Come in,' said Katie.

The door opened, and there stood Ribby Ratsoup, Wily Winnie's cat.

'Good morning,' she said, trying to curtsey politely, but it was difficult because she was wearing riding-boots and carried a large bucket over one paw.

'Good morning,' said Katie. 'If you've brought that

bucket for salt herrings, you can spare yourself the trouble; you're not having any.'

'No, no, nothing of the kind!' said the cat. 'I just called to see if anyone here would like to go bilberry-picking with me.'

'Bilberry-picking?' said Gapy Gob. 'You going bilberry-picking? What a clever cat you are! But I don't think Katie and Charlie have time to go with you today.' The ogre was a bit put out because he had had to wait for his porridge.

'I was just asking,' said Ribby in a sugary voice. 'You see, at *our* house we get up early. I get all the work done before breakfast. So my mistress told me to go berrying today, and of course I do as I am told. Well, bye-bye for now!'

When the cat had gone, the ogre said, 'I don't really see why you shouldn't go bilberrying too; they're very nice to eat. . . .' And he licked his chops.

'Just as you like,' said Charlie. 'We don't mind going. But then you'll have to look after yourself while we're out.'

'Don't touch the matches, whatever you do!' warned Katie.

'And if anybody knocks, be sure *not* to open the door,' said Charlie.

'I won't,' said Gapy Gob.

But as soon as the children had gone, Wily Winnie came panting over the hill, her skirts flying.

'Hullo, hullo! How are you, Gapy Gob?' she shouted, and marched straight into the kitchen.

Gapy Gob backed away from her into a corner. 'I'm not supposed to open the door if anyone knocks,' he said.

'Ah, but I *didn't* knock. I came straight in!' said the ogress. 'How nice to see you again, dear Gapy Gob. My cat has gone bilberry-picking, so I was all alone!'

'The children have gone as well,' said Gapy Gob.

'How lovely!' cried Wily Winnie. 'Then you can come home with me for a while. We can sit and talk while we wait for them to bring back the berries. I wonder who will bring the most? Come along now, Gapy, let me help you on with your coat. First this arm; that's right, and now this one. There now, we're ready to go!'

So Gapy Gob went home with Wily Winnie and sat in her house all day, while Katie Cook and Charlie Chop searched the wood for all the bilberries they could find. They each had a punnet to pick in, and when they were full they tipped them into their bucket which stood under a fir-tree.

But what d'you think Ribby Ratsoup had been doing all this time? Well, she hadn't been picking bilberries, I

can tell you that much! She spent the day scampering through the forest, chasing squirrels and field mice and birds. Late in the afternoon she came across the children's bucket, filled almost to the brim with bilberries. Katie and Charlie were out of sight, picking their last punnet each.

Ribby, as I told you before, was a very cunning cat. She emptied all the berries into her own bucket and one of her boots. Ther. she ran home to her mistress as fast as she could go.

Back in Wily Winnie's house the ogre and ogress were getting on fine together. They had come to an agreement that if the *cat* came home with most bilberries, Gapy

Gob would send Katie and Charlie away, but if the *children* had most, Ribby Ratsoup would have to go.

Suddenly they saw something come streaking across the hill-top. It was the cat with her bucket and her boot full of bilberries.

Wily Winnie clapped her hands. 'My cat's won! My cat's won! Look what a lot she's brought!'

'Ah, you wait and see what the children bring!' said Gapy Gob. He was so fond of the children, he didn't want to lose them.

A little while later they saw Katie and Charlie come over the hill-top. But they were walking very, very slowly. And their bucket was—empty.

'What did I tell you, Gapy Gob?' shouted the ogress. 'Those children are no good. Send them away, Gapy, send them away!'

So Gapy Gob went out in the yard and said to the

children: 'Charlie and Katie, you can go. I don't want you any more; you can't even pick bilberries.' And he turned away, for he had tears in his eyes.

'I see,' said Charlie.

'Very well,' said Katie.

'Ribby is much better at picking than you are,' said Gapy Gob.

'Is that so?' said Charlie. 'Then perhaps Madam Ratsoup wouldn't mind showing us her paws?'

'My paws?' said the cat. 'Certainly you can see my paws.' And she held them up.

'Hmm!' said Charlie. 'Very strange. The cat has picked a whole bucket and a boot full, yet her paws are as clean as if she'd been licking them all day. *We*, who have no bilberries to show for it, have our arms stained blue right up to the elbows. Ribby Ratsoup is a thief; she has stolen our berries and now she can give them back to us, every single one, or it will be the worse for her!'

The cat saw the game was up and quickly handed back the berries. Then the children took Gapy Gob by the hands and they all three went home together.

But Wily Winnie was so angry, she shut the cat up in the barn without any supper.

That's the end of this story. Now it's your turn to make one up about the ogres, and we'll see which is the best.

The good luck story

ONCE upon a time there was a little old woman—no, what am I saying? She was a little girl. But this little girl worked every bit as hard as any grown-up woman. Her name was Betsy; she wore a scarf round her head like the women did, and she could weed a field of turnips with the best of them. If any of the big boys started throwing stones or lumps of earth at her, she tossed her head and gave them a piece of her mind.

She was weeding in the field one day when a ladybird settled on her hand.

'Poor little ladybird! What do you want on my thumb?' said Betsy, at the same time trying to think of a really good wish. For ever since she was tiny she had been told to make a wish when a ladybird flew from her finger.

'I wish . . . I wish I had a new skipping-rope to take to school,' she said quickly. But then she remembered that she had borrowed a skipping-rope from her friend, Anna, and lost it. If she got a new one now she would *have* to give it to Anna.

The ladybird crawled slowly out on Betsy's thumb-nail, and she was terrified it would fly away before she had had time to wish for all the things she wanted. Luckily, the ladybird changed its mind when it reached the top; it crawled down again and started up the first finger.

'Now I shall wish—I wish I could have some money,' said Betsy, but was sorry as soon as she had said it. After all, she would *get* some money when she had finished her weeding. And, anyway, the money would have to go to Britta from Hill Farm to pay for the old bicycle Betsy had bought from her in the spring.

The ladybird crawled right out on the top of Betsy's first finger. Then it stopped to consider, and slowly

turned round and climbed down again to start on the second finger.

'Now I must hurry up and wish before it flies off the top of this finger,' said Betsy, while the ladybird climbed steadily upwards.

'I wish I were a real princess,' she said, but then she thought: 'How stupid of me—how can I be a real princess if I haven't been one before? Unless, of course, a prince came along and asked me to marry him. That would look funny, wouldn't it? A prince in a turnip field!' And she laughed at herself.

The ladybird was stretching one wing now and hovering.

'Don't fly yet, little ladybird! I don't want to be a princess at all. I want something quite different. I want my mother to be rid of her rheumatics when I get home tonight.'

This was a good wish, and Betsy was pleased with it. You see, it was a great trouble to her when her mother had the rheumatics; then Betsy had to dress all her little brothers and sisters and give them their dinner. It would be nice not to have to work so hard.

But the ladybird didn't take off even from this finger. Slowly it turned round and made its way to the bottom of the finger and then on to Betsy's hand. Then it stopped; it didn't seem to want to go on at all. But Betsy gave it a gentle little push and got it on to her third finger.

Now she knew what to wish; that her father could get the job he was after that day. Because if he did, he had said he would buy her a whole sheet of pictures to stick in her scrap-book.

But the ladybird had its own ideas; it crawled more and more slowly up Betsy's third finger, and every now and then Betsy had to poke it to get it out on the nail. Then all of a sudden the ladybird rolled off and fell on to the ground.

Betsy lay down flat among the turnips and managed to coax the creature on to her little finger. It didn't move. So Betsy lifted it gingerly out on the nail. Still it didn't move, and she thought she must have hurt it. 'You poor thing! Did I squeeze you too hard? Oh, please, little ladybird, do fly now! Because I want to wish that Daddy could get the job he's after!'

And suddenly the ladybird opened its wings and flew off—straight up towards the sun.

And do you know? When Betsy got home that night her mother was feeling better than she had been for a long while. Her father had got the job and had remembered the pictures for her scrap-book, and her friend Anna had been to see her. She had found the lost skipping-rope and brought it for Betsy, because she had a new one herself. Not only that, but Britta from Hill Farm had been to say that if Betsy would mind her baby for her twice that week, she needn't pay any more for the old bicycle!

What more could you want from a lucky ladybird?

Mr. Big Toe's journey

MR. BIG TOE lived with his four brothers in a little sock, and the sock lived in a shoe which belonged to a little boy who was walking down the lane eating a very big sandwich.

Mr. Big Toe said: 'Now I've been stuck in this place so long, I think it's time I did some travelling.'

When his brothers asked him where he was going, he answered: 'Oh, I expect I shall sail across the ocean.'

'But how will you get through the wall?' they asked him—they meant the sock, of course.

'That's easy for someone as big as I am. I shall just scratch a hole.'

'Will we never see you again?' asked the one who was closest to Mr. Big Toe.

'Maybe not. But I'll ring you up and tell you how I'm getting on. Well, I'm off now, so goodbye!'

Then Mr. Big Toe started scratching a hole, and it didn't take long before he had wriggled through. The rest of the toes sat waiting for the telephone message.

Soon the little boy started running and Mr. Big Toe sent his first message:

'Hullo, hullo! I've started on my travels. It feels rather strange at first, of course, and I miss you a bit. But I expect you miss me much more. Be good. I'll ring you up again when I get on the boat.'

After a time the little boy found a puddle and began dipping his shoe in it. Mr. Big Toe got on the telephone again.

'Hullo boys, I've just got to the edge of the ocean; in a few moments I'll be sailing to the far shore. It's a dangerous journey, but don't worry, I'll manage! The waves are enormous! Still, the boat seems strong and seaworthy. It won't be long now before I meet the African Chief's Big Toe and all his little black brothers. I'll tell them I've left *my* four brothers at home. They'll be glad to hear about you, I expect. . . . Bye, bye, I must ring off now till we get to the far shore.'

The boy waded out into the middle of the puddle, but it was deeper than he thought, and while the other toes were lying inside the sock, thinking of their big brother alone on the stormy sea, they had another call from him.

'Hullo there! This is getting more and more dangerous; the boat is out in the middle of the ocean, and it's leaking badly. If you don't hear anything more for a

bit, it's because I have to use my nail to bail the water out. It's difficult, but I'm not a bit afraid!'

'Poor Big Toe!' the brothers said to each other and huddled closer together inside the sock.

The little boy had splashed through the puddle by now. Next he found a tricycle and got on it. He rode it as fast as he could and stuck both his legs straight out in the air.

Mr. Big Toe's telephone rang again. 'Hullo boys, hullo! It's your brother Big Toe calling. I'm floating in mid-air. I'm in an aeroplane, but you needn't worry, it's quite safe. The boat sank, though I did my best to bail all the water out. I was alone, you see, that made it very difficult. However, you'll be pleased to know I'm on my way home now. See you all soon!'

The boy went indoors to change his wet socks. The five toes got a new home to live in and the boy set out again with another big sandwich in his hand.

'Fancy you coming home to us!' said all the brothers to Mr. Big Toe, and they curled themselves round him to make him feel warm and cosy.

'Yes, yes, home is all right when the sock is dry and clean,' said Mr. Big Toe. 'But I don't suppose it will be long before I take another journey.'

A concertina concert

Do you remember the story we made up? The one about the ogres, Gapy Gob and Wily Winnie? Gapy Gob had two servants, Katie Cook and Charlie Chop, who were not ogres at all, but just ordinary children. Wily Winnie had a cat to look after her, called Ribby Ratsoup, a very cunning cat. These two would sit at home in the evenings and talk about how they could get Gapy Gob to marry Wily Winnie. Then one day, just after New Year, the cat had an idea.

'I know how to get Gapy Gob to marry you,' she said. 'Tell him you have learned to play the concertina. Gapy likes concertina music better than anything.'

'You have some bright ideas, I must say!' said Wily Winnie scornfully. 'You know I can't play the concertina.'

'Don't worry about that,' said Ribby. 'I met a musician in the forest this morning; that's what made me think of it. Wait here till I fetch him.'

So the cat went into the forest and there, under a fir-tree, sat a very small, thin musician. He had been

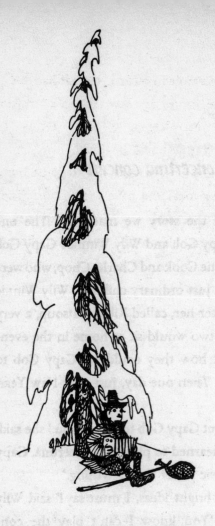

playing his concertina at village gatherings all through Christmas and now he was anxious to get home as quickly as possible. But when Ribby had met him that morning, the little musician had lost his way in the forest. So Ribby had promised to come back and guide him if he would wait there.

'You can play me a tune in return,' the cat had said.

Now, when the musician saw the cat trotting towards him he was very pleased.

'Shall I play you a tune now?' he asked.

'Not just yet,' said Ribby. 'I want you to come home with me first to eat a meal and have some coffee. Then you can play your concertina to me and my mistress.'

This sounded a good idea to the musician, who was hungry by now. But when he got to the door and saw that the cat's mistress was an ogress, he was very frightened.

At first Wily Winnie did her best to be nice to him, but as this only made him more frightened, she ordered Ribby to lock the door. 'Now,' she said to the little musician, 'you'll do as we say!' And she brought out a large orange-box and put it in the middle of the floor.

'Get in that box, quick sharp!' said the ogress. And the musician had to crawl inside, whether he liked it or not.

Then Wily Winnie said: 'You're to stay in that box and not make a sound until I give the box a kick. Then you must play "A Life on the Ocean Wave" on your concertina.'

'Do I have to sing as well?' asked the musician, whose knees were knocking together with fear.

'Certainly,' said Wily Winnie. 'What's more, you've to make up a song about Gapy Gob and me this instant

—something about how I love him and would like him
to marry me.'

The musician thought as quickly as he could, and
then he sang this song:

> 'Gapy Gob is bright and fair,
> Combing down his yellow hair,
> He's my ain for ever mair,
> Bonny Gapy Gob—o!'

'Not my own idea, I'm afraid,' said the musician,
'but it's rather difficult to make up songs sitting in an
orange-box.'

'It'll do,' said Wily Winnie. Then she sent the cat to
fetch Gapy Gob, and smartened herself up as well as she
could. Suddenly she remembered she would have to
have a concertina herself, or Gapy Gob would never
believe she was playing it.

'I must have a concertina,' she said.

'You'll find an old broken one in my sack,' said the musician. 'It hasn't a note in it.'

'Good,' said Wily Winnie. So she sat down and waited for Ribby to come back with Gapy Gob. But they were a very long time.

'I think I shall have to go and see what has happened to my cat,' said the ogress. 'You wait there.' And she left the musician sitting in the box. He hadn't been there long, however, before the door opened. Can you guess who came in? Katie Cook and Charlie Chop.

When the cat had arrived to invite Gapy Gob to come and listen to Wily Winnie playing the concertina, the children were quite sure something was up. So they had slipped out the back way and taken a short cut through the forest to the ogress's house. They had just seen Wily Winnie leave so they knew it was safe to go in.

'I wonder what's in that orange-box?' said Charlie Chop.

'It's me!' said the musician, and he told the children the whole story of what had happened to him after he had got lost.

'I'll show you the way home,' said Katie, 'but we'll have to be quick; the others will be here any moment now. Follow me!'

The musician crawled out of the box and ran out of the house with Katie as fast as his thin legs could carry him.

Charlie had borrowed the good concertina; now he crept into the box in the musician's place.

After a time the cat came back with Wily Winnie and Gapy Gob. The ogress was in high spirits. 'Now you just listen, Gapy Gob,' she said. 'I'm going to sit on this orange-box and play "A Life on the Ocean Wave" and you'll be *amazed*.' She picked up the old broken concertina, gave the box a kick, and started pretending to play.

But what came out was *not* 'A Life on the Ocean Wave' because, of course, it was Charlie Chop who was inside the box, and he made the most horrible noise he could on the concertina.

'Oh no, please stop!' said Gapy Gob, holding his ears. 'That was the most frightful noise I ever heard!'

'Perhaps you would like me to sing for you instead,' said Wily Winnie, and gave the box another kick. This was the signal for the musician to sing his song about Gapy Gob—you know, the one that went like 'Bobby Shaftoe':

'Gapy Gob is bright and fair,
Combing down his yellow hair,
He's my ain for ever mair,
Bonny Gapy Gob—o!'

But this is what Charlie sang instead:

'Gapy is the ugliest fellow,
Ever since I first could bellow,
I have wished he was a toad
So I could chase him down the road.'

'Well!' said Gapy Gob. 'I must say! If you've brought me all this way to make a fool of me, I'll go home this minute, and that's flat! Toad, indeed!' And with that he stumped out of the house, slamming the door behind him.

'Wait, Gapy! Dear Gapy! I can explain!' wailed the ogress as she hurried after him. Charlie Chop took this chance to get out of the box and run home by the short cut.

All this time Ribby Ratsoup had been in the kitchen cooking a celebration feast for his mistress and Gapy Gob. She couldn't understand why everything was so quiet suddenly, so she came in to have a look. There was nobody there. Not even in the orange-box, though she got inside it to make sure.

Just at that moment Wily Winnie came back; she was *not* in high spirits *now*. 'So it's you who's been sitting in there mocking me!' she shouted. 'You wait till I get my broom! I'll give you the hiding of your life!'

Late that night, when the little musician had long since reached home, and Gapy Gob had had his supper, and Katie Cook and Charlie Chop had finished all their work for the day, two dark figures could be seen leaping from hill-top to hill-top; it was Wily Winnie chasing Ribby Ratsoup with her broom.

A birthday party in Topsy Turvy Town

IN TOPSY TURVY TOWN, where the sun rises in the West and goes down in the North, and three times fourteen is four, the Mayor was going to have his fiftieth birthday. His little girl, Trixie, was busy baking cakes, but she couldn't get on, because the Mayor *would* keep bothering her to know how much longer it would be before his birthday.

'Do stop bothering me, Daddy dear,' she said. 'When you've slept one more night it will be your birthday. So run along to your office now, please, and write out invitations to the people you want to come to your party.'

'I won't ask the Postmaster, anyway,' said the Mayor.

'Why ever not?'

'He always teases me about my big ears,' answered the Mayor.

'That's only when he's with the Smith,' said Trixie. 'You always play perfectly well when the Smith isn't there.'

'But I want to ask the Smith,' said the Mayor. 'I'm sure he'll behave if he knows we're having birthday cake.'

'Well, you'd better ask them both, then.'

'I want to ask the Doctor and the Dentist as well,' said the Mayor.

'I only hope the Doctor will be well enough to go out,' said Trixie. 'I spoke to his little girl yesterday, and she

told me he had had a very bad night, tossing and turning. She was afraid he might be sickening for something. But I expect you'd better ask him all the same.'

'Oh yes, otherwise he'd sulk,' said the Mayor. 'So would the Dentist.'

'You do as you like,' said Trixie, 'but you know he isn't allowed any sweet things like chocolate cake with icing on.'

'I know. But we could give him apples and rusks instead,' said the Mayor.

'That's a good idea. Are you asking any more?'

'What a question! I can't leave the Baker out, can I?'

'Now, now, that's not the way for a Mayor to talk to his little girl!' said Trixie. 'Anyway, if you ask him you can't have any more; there isn't room.' Then she told him to put the invitations through the letter-boxes and come straight home to bed to have a good sleep before the great day.

The next day the Mayor was very excited. He sat in his office and looked at the clock till it was time to go home. Then he raced back to put on his Grand Chain of Office and went and stood by the door to welcome his guests.

The first to arrive was the Smith. He had his hands in his pockets.

'Many Happy Returns of the Day,' he said.

'Thank you,' said the Mayor, holding out his hand for the present.

'Haven't brought a present,' said the Smith.

'Never mind,' said Trixie soothingly. 'Wouldn't you like to take off those big heavy boots before you come in?'

'No,' said the Smith.

'Why not?' asked the little girl.

'Hole in my sock,' said the Smith.

'You can borrow my daddy's slippers. And then what about taking your hands out of your pockets?'

'No,' said the Smith.

'Why not?'

'Dirty,' said the Smith.

'Oh, we'll soon deal with that!' said Trixie. 'You come along to the bathroom with me; I'll help you

wash them. You'll have to let the others in by yourself, Daddy dear.'

Next came the Doctor and the Dentist. They walked hand-in-hand and each had a little parcel under his arm.

'Many Happy Returns,' they said, both together.

'Thank you very much,' said the Mayor, and started

unwrapping. The Doctor's present was a stethoscope, but it was only a toy, because it was broken. The Dentist gave him a nice thing to squirt his mouth with.

Then came the Postmaster, and he brought a packet

of stamps which were very unusual, because all the edges had been cut off.

Last of all came the Baker. He brought a large slab of chocolate, and when he had wished the Mayor many happy returns he broke the chocolate in two, gave one half to the Mayor and stuffed the other half in his pocket.

'Come in, all of you,' Trixie said, as she came out of the bathroom with the Smith. His hands were now so clean, he was ashamed to show them.

In the dining-room there was a fine spread, with a huge birthday cake in the middle of the table decorated with fifty candles.

'Now do sit down and help yourselves,' invited Trixie. 'I'm just going to telephone.' And she shut the door. She picked up the receiver. 'Hullo, can you please give me the little girl in Flat 2?'

'There you are,' said the operator.

'Hullo, is that you, Kitty? This is Trixie.'

'Oh, hullo Trixie! What do you want?'

'Could you come and help me this afternoon? My daddy is having a birthday party and there *is* so much to do!'

'Yes, all right. But I'll have to bring my doll's ironing; there's a whole heap of it,' said Kitty on the telephone.

'We can iron together, then. *I* have a whole heap to do as well,' said Trixie.

As she put the 'phone down, Trixie heard a terrible crash from the dining-room, and when she opened the door what a sight met her eyes! There was birthday cake plastered all over the walls, and cups and saucers were strewn about the floor!

'What is the meaning of this?' she demanded sternly.

It was the Postmaster who answered. 'Well, you see, the Mayor tried to blow out the candles and he couldn't do it, so we all had a go and none of us could do it. Except the Smith.'

Trixie frowned. 'How did *you* manage it when the others couldn't do it?' she asked.

'Had my bellows,' said the Smith, staring up at the ceiling.

'Oh dear,' sighed Trixie. 'I suppose I shall have to clean up the mess. But then you really must behave. I have someone coming to see me, and we shall be in the nursery. So you're not to come in there. You can play in the sitting-room when you have finished your tea.' Then she left them to get on with it.

Trixie and her friend Kitty were ironing their dolls' clothes and having a very interesting talk together when suddenly there was another awful crash from the room where the party was going on. The Mayor came and knocked on the nursery door.

'What is it?' asked Trixie.

'It's the Postmaster,' said the Mayor; 'he's started teasing me again; I want him to go home.'

Trixie had to go and make peace. 'I really don't know why you can't play nicely instead of quarrelling,' she said.

The Postmaster was standing next to the Smith, staring at the floor. The Smith was looking at the ceiling, as usual.

'What did the Postmaster say?' asked Trixie.

'He said my ears were so big he would put a stamp on my forehead and send me by air-mail,' said the Mayor.

'*We* never put stamps on people and send them by air-mail,' said the Doctor and the Dentist, both together.

'Oh, how silly!' said Trixie. 'Now please be good boys and play a game, or something. What about Blind Man's Buff? Then I'll go and cook some lovely hot sausages for you.'

Trixie called to Kitty. 'I'll have to stop ironing dolls' clothes now, I must cook the sausages.'

'I'll come and help you,' said Kitty. 'I've finished my ironing.'

'Good,' said Trixie. But no sooner had they got to work in the kitchen than the door of the sitting-room flew open, and the Baker rushed out, grabbing his coat from the peg. Then he shot through the front door and down the main stairs, taking two at a time.

'*Now* what's happened?' asked Trixie.

The Mayor, who was nearly crying, came out in the kitchen. 'The Baker snatched his present back and ran off, just because he couldn't catch any of us in Blind Man's Buff,' he said.

'Oh dear! Oh dear!' said Trixie.

'*We* don't snatch our presents back and run off home,' said the Doctor and the Dentist.

'Of course not. You're *good* boys,' said Trixie, 'and I have some nice hot sausages for you.' Suddenly she noticed the Dentist's face. 'Goodness Gracious!' she exclaimed. 'What's that swelling you have on your cheek?' She beckoned to Kitty to have a look. 'I do believe he's got an ab—ab—what's it called?'

'You mean an abscess,' said Kitty, who was very clever. She climbed on the Dentist's knee. The Dentist opened his mouth wide, and, sure enough, he had an abscess!

'You'll have to go home to your little girl at once,' said Trixie, 'and get her to pull out the tooth for you.'

'He's not the only one who'll have to go home,' said Kitty. 'Look at the Doctor, he's coming out in spots all over his face. I expect he's getting measles.'

'Goodness Gracious!' cried Trixie. 'You'll all have to go at once before you catch the measles. Hurry and get your things on!'

So they all put on their coats and shook hands and said 'thank you' before they went home.

All except the Smith. He sat in the hall and took a very long time to put on his boots.

'You must go home to *your* little girl now,' said Trixie.

'Haven't got one,' said the Smith, with his eyes on the ceiling.

Trixie and Kitty both said 'Oh, you poor thing!' and they gave him all that was left of the birthday cake and a bucket, full of sausages, to take home.

The Mayor walked round the dining-room table, scraping all the plates and drinking all the cold tea. He thought it had been a wonderful party.

Father Christmas and the carpenter

THERE was once a carpenter called Anderson. He was a good father and he had a lot of children.

One Christmas Eve, while his wife and children were decorating the Christmas tree, Anderson crept out to his wood-shed. He had a surprise for them all: he was going to dress up as Father Christmas, load a sack of presents on to his sledge and go and knock on the front door. But as he pulled the loaded sledge out of the wood-shed, he slipped and fell right across the sack of presents. This set the sledge moving, because the ground sloped from the shed down to the road, and Anderson had no time even to shout 'Way there!' before he crashed into another sledge which was coming down the road.

'I'm very sorry,' said Anderson.

'Don't mention it; I couldn't stop myself,' said the other man. Like Anderson, he was dressed in Father Christmas clothes and had a sack on his sledge.

'We seem to have had the same idea,' said Anderson. 'I see you're all dressed up like me.' He laughed and shook the other man's hand. 'My name's Anderson.'

'Glad to meet you,' said the other. 'I'm Father Christmas.'

'Ha, ha!' laughed Anderson. 'You will have your little joke, and quite right too on a Christmas Eve.'

'That's what I thought,' said the other man, 'and if you agree we can change places tonight, and that will be a better joke still; I'll take the presents along to *your* children, if you'll go and visit *mine*. But you must take off that costume.'

Anderson looked a bit puzzled. 'What am I to dress up in then?'

'You don't need to dress up at all,' said the other. 'My children see Father Christmas all the year round, but they've never seen a real carpenter. I told them last Christmas that if they were good this year I'd try and get the carpenter to come and see them while I went round with presents for the human children.'

'So he really *is* Father Christmas,' thought Anderson to himself. Out loud he said: 'All right, if you really want me to, I will. The only thing is, I haven't any presents for your children.'

'Presents?' said Father Christmas. 'Aren't you a carpenter?'

'Yes, of course.'

'Well, then, all you have to do is to take along a few pieces of wood and some nails. You have a knife, I suppose?' Anderson said he had and went to look for the things in his workshop.

'Just follow my footsteps in the snow; they'll lead you to my house in the forest,' said Father Christmas. 'Then I'll take your sack and sledge and go and knock on your door.

'Righto!' said the carpenter.

Then Father Christmas went off to knock at Anderson's door, and the carpenter trudged through the

snow in Father Christmas's footsteps. They led him into
the forest, past two pine-trees, a large boulder and a
tree-stump. There, peeping out from behind the stump,
were three little faces with red caps on.

'He's here! He's here!' shouted the Christmas children as they scampered in front of him to a fallen tree,
lying with its roots in the air. When Anderson followed
them round to the other side of the roots he found
Mother Christmas standing there waiting for him.

'Here he is, Mum! Here's the carpenter Dad promised
us! Look at him! Isn't he tall!' The children were all
shouting at once.

'Now, now, children,' said Mother Christmas, 'anybody would think you'd never seen a human being
before.'

'We've never seen a proper *carpenter* before!' shouted
the children. 'Come on in, Mr. Carpenter!'

Pulling a branch aside, Mother Christmas led the way
into the house. Anderson had to bend his long back
double and crawl on his hands and knees. But once in,
he found he could straighten up. The room had a mud
floor, but it was very cosy, with tree-stumps for chairs,
and beds made of moss with covers of plaited grass. In
the smallest bed lay the Christmas baby and in the far
corner sat a very old Grandfather Christmas, his red cap
nodding up and down.

'Have you got a knife? Did you bring some wood and some nails?' The children wanted to know everything at once and pulled at Anderson's sleeve.

'Now, children,' said Mother Christmas, 'let the carpenter sit down before you start pestering him.'

'Has anyone come to see me?' croaked old Grandfather Christmas.

Mother Christmas shouted in his ear. 'It's Anderson, the carpenter!' She explained that Grandfather was so old he never went out any more. 'He'd be pleased if you came over and shook hands with him.'

So Anderson took the old man's hand which was as hard as a piece of bark.

'Come and sit here, Mr. Carpenter!' called the children.

The eldest one spoke first. 'D'you know what I want you to make for me? A toboggan. Can you do that—a little one, I mean?'

'I'll try,' said Anderson, and it didn't take long before he had a smart toboggan just ready to fly over the snow.

'Now it's my turn,' said the little girl who had pig-tails sticking straight out from her head. 'I want a doll's bed.'

'Have you any dolls?' asked Anderson.

'No, but I borrow the field-mice sometimes, and I can play with the baby squirrels as much as I like. They *love* being dolls. Please make me a doll's bed.'

So the carpenter made her a doll's bed. Then he asked the smaller boy what he would like. But he was very shy and could only whisper, 'Don't know.'

' 'Course he knows!' said his sister. 'He said it just before you came. Go on, tell the carpenter.'

'A top,' whispered the little boy.

'That's easy,' said the carpenter, and in no time at all he had made a top.

'And now you must make something for Mum!' said the children. Mother Christmas had been watching, but all the time she held something behind her back.

'Shush, children, don't keep bothering the carpenter,' she said.

'That's all right,' said Anderson. 'What would you like me to make?'

Mother Christmas brought out the thing she was holding; it was a wooden ladle, very worn, with a crack in it.

'Could you mend this for me, d'you think?' she asked.

'Hm, hm!' said Anderson, scratching his ear with his carpenter's pencil. 'I think I'd better make you a new one.' And he quickly cut a new ladle for Mother Christmas. Then he found a long twisted root with a crook at

one end and started stripping it with his knife. But, although the children asked him and asked him, he wouldn't tell them what it was going to be. When it was finished he held it up; it was a very distinguished-looking walking-stick.

'Here you are, Grandpa!' he shouted to the old man, and handed him the stick. Then he gathered up all the chips and made a wonderful little bird with wings outspread to hang over the baby's cot.

'How pretty!' exclaimed Mother Christmas and all the children. 'Thank the carpenter nicely now. We'll certainly never forget this Christmas Eve, will we?'

'Thank you, Mr. Carpenter, thank you very much!' shouted the children.

Grandfather Christmas himself came stumping across the room, leaning on his new stick. 'It's grand!' he said. 'It's just grand!'

There was a sound of feet stamping the snow off outside the door, and Anderson knew it was time for him to go. He said goodbye all round and wished them a Happy Christmas. Then he crawled through the narrow opening under the fallen tree. Father Christmas was waiting for him. He had the sledge and the empty sack with him.

'Thank you for your help, Anderson,' he said. 'What did the youngsters say when they saw you?'

'Oh, they seemed very pleased. Now they're just waiting for you to come home and see their new toys. How did you get on at my house? Was little Peter frightened of you?'

'Not a bit,' said Father Christmas. 'He thought I was you. "Sit on Dadda's knee," he kept saying.'

'Well, I must get back to them,' said Anderson, and said goodbye to Father Christmas.

When he got home, the first thing he said to the children was, 'Can I see the presents you got from Father Christmas?'

But the children laughed. 'Silly! You've seen them already—when you were Father Christmas; you un-packed them all for us!'

'What would you say if I told you I had been with Father Christmas's family all this time?'

But the children laughed again. 'You wouldn't say anything so silly!' they said, and they didn't believe him. So the carpenter came to me and asked me to write the story down, which I did.

Mrs Pepperpot's Outing
and other stories

As Mr Pepperpot passed the place where he had spilt the first ice-cream, he made the mistake of looking down. And do you know? The ice-cream on the ground was *moving*! Poor Mr Pepperpot dropped the second cornet on the first one and fled back to the kiosk. He was sure there was a snake in the grass, and he was very much afraid of snakes.

And what was going on down there in the grass where two double ice-creams were bubbling and churning like porridge on the boil? You've guessed it. Mrs Pepperpot was underneath! She had got out of the car to stretch her legs, and then, suddenly, she had SHRUNK to the size of a pepperpot!

Alf Prøysen

Mrs PEPPERPOT'S OUTING

Translated by Marianne Helweg
Illustrated by Bjorn Berg

Contents

Mrs Pepperpot's Outing

I

IT was a beautiful sunny summer morning, and Mrs
Pepperpot was standing at her kitchen window peeling
onions. You remember Mrs Pepperpot? She's the little
old woman who lives on a hillside in Norway and has the
habit of shrinking to the size of a pepperpot at the most
inconvenient moments.

Well, here she was, peeling onions, and from time to time she sniffed a little, the way people do when they are peeling onions. As the tears rolled down her cheeks she wiped them away with the back of her hand and sighed. She was not feeling very happy.

But Mr Pepperpot was; he was on holiday. Now he came rushing through the door with his hat askew, and his hair all over the place. Waving his arms, he shouted: 'I've good news for you, Mrs P! Guess what it is.'

'Good news?' said Mrs Pepperpot. 'Have you found me a new pet?' Because she had just been thinking how empty and sad the house was without even a cat or a dog.

'No, no, something *much* better. You'll have to have another guess,' said her husband. 'Pets! How can you be so old-fashioned? They're a dead loss when you want to go away anywhere, always needing to be fed and looked after.'

'But I *like* looking after animals; they're fun,' she answered. 'Besides, quite often one doesn't really *want* to go away, and then it's very useful to be able to say you have to look after the animals.' She wiped away another tear: 'Oh, those onions!'

'Well, I think you're behind the times,' said Mr Pepperpot. 'It's good for everyone to get about and not be stuck in one place all your life.'

This made Mrs Pepperpot laugh. 'Did you say get about? How far do we get in your old wreck of a car? The person who's stuck in one place is *you* with your head under the bonnet every night for weeks on end!'

'It's my hobby,' said Mr Pepperpot. 'Everyone should have a hobby nowadays. It says in the paper you should make good use of your free time.'

You see, Mr Pepperpot had bought an old car cheaply, and ever since he had been tinkering with it, putting in new parts and cleaning and polishing it.

'You still haven't guessed my news, so I'll tell you,' he said. 'We're going for an outing in the car!'

'You mean you've really got it working?' Mrs Pepperpot could hardly believe it. 'Where are we going?'

'There's a car rally over the other side of Blocksberg: it's for old cars, so I thought I might enter mine. I might even win a cup.'

This was a sore point with Mr Pepperpot. His wife knew

9

he had always wanted to win a cup or a trophy. They did have one in the house, but she kept it hidden at the back of a cupboard, because it was one *she* had won when she was a young girl, and worked on a farm. She had got it for being so good at looking after the livestock. Now she would really like Mr Pepperpot to have one too, so she said:

'Yes, let's go. An outing would be fun, and we can take a picnic.'

'I'll just go and check the engine once more; be ready in half an hour.'

Mrs Pepperpot bustled about; she was quite looking forward to seeing some new places after the long winter at home. She got out the picnic basket, hard-boiled some

eggs, packed bread and butter and a piece of cold ham and some pancakes left over from last night. As she worked she made up a little song to sing in the car. This is how it went, to the tune of 'Nuts in May':

'My hubby is mad about motoring,
Motoring, motoring,
He spends his evenings tinkering
On his rickety automobile.

So now we'll be bouncing up and down
Up and down, up and down,
Everything in the back seat is thrown
Off the rickety automobile!

I may be crazy to go with him,
Go with him, go with him,
But oh, he's made it look so trim,
His rickety automobile!

At least we'll have a fine picnic,
A fine picnic, a fine picnic,
With sausages, bread and ham and chick
In his rickety automobile!

And then of course we'll see the sights,
See the sights, see the sights,
Of valleys and forests and mountain heights
From his rickety automobile!

Hooray!'

Mr Pepperpot grumbled when she brought the loaded basket out to the car. 'What do we want with all that stuff? Much better to buy ice-cream as we go along and there are plenty of cafés where we can have a hot-dog and ketchup.' He liked to show that he knew what tourists did when they went motoring.

'No nourishment in ice-cream,' said Mrs Pepperpot. 'And I don't trust cafés.' With that she dumped the basket in the back seat and got in.

Mr Pepperpot got in the driving seat. But just before he started the engine he had a sudden thought: 'You won't *shrink* while we're out, will you?'

'Oh, stop fussing!' said Mrs Pepperpot, as she settled herself comfortably. 'You know I never have any idea when it's going to happen. If it does, it does, and I usually manage, don't I? Start up, Mr P, I'm quite looking forward to this outing!'

So off they went. At first Mr Pepperpot drove very carefully down the little country road from the house. But once they were on the main road, with its smooth asphalt surface, he put his foot on the pedal and they hummed along at quite a good pace. He started to whistle; Mr Pepperpot always did that when he was happy.

'This is the life!' he sang. 'All these years I've been mucking about with an old horse and cart, never getting

anywhere, never seeing anything.'

'I don't know,' said Mrs Pepperpot. 'You used to get around quite well on a bicycle—fast enough to break your neck!'

'Yes, but think of the advantages of a motor-car: four wheels, comfortable seats, plenty of room for luggage and a roof to keep the rain out.'

'Plenty of expense too,' answered Mrs Pepperpot, 'and plenty of time needed for repairs. When will you ever get around to clearing the drains or help me dig up potatoes now?'

'Stop grumbling and enjoy yourself!' ordered Mr Pepperpot as he slowed down over a little bridge. On the other side there was a kiosk selling ice-cream.

'There, didn't I tell you we could get ice-cream?' said

Mr Pepperpot. 'I'll go and get you one.' So he hopped out of the car and went over to the kiosk to buy a double vanilla cornet for Mrs Pepperpot. 'That should put her in a good mood,' he said to himself, as he balanced his way back towards the car with it. But half-way there he was distracted by a hissing noise in the grass at his feet.

'Oops!' he said, and dropped the beautiful ice-cream!

There was nothing for it but to go back for another. He paid his money and the girl gave him a second ice-cream as big as the first. Back he went, holding the cornet with its great mound on top very steady. But as he passed the place where he had spilt the first one, he made the mistake of looking down. And do you know? The ice-

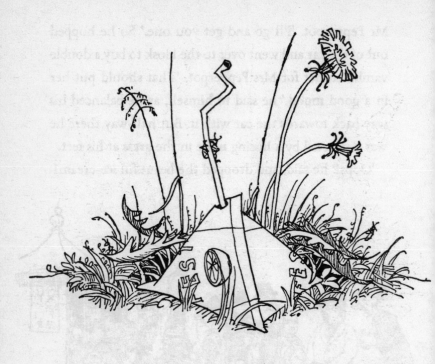

cream on the ground was *moving*! Poor Mr Pepperpot dropped the second cornet on the first one and fled back to the kiosk. He was sure there was a snake in the grass, and he was very much afraid of snakes.

But back at the kiosk a bus-load of trippers had just lined up for refreshments and Mr Pepperpot had to stand at the end of the queue.

And what was going on down there in the grass where two double ice-creams were bubbling and churning like porridge on the boil? You've guessed it: Mrs Pepperpot was underneath! She had got out of the car to stretch

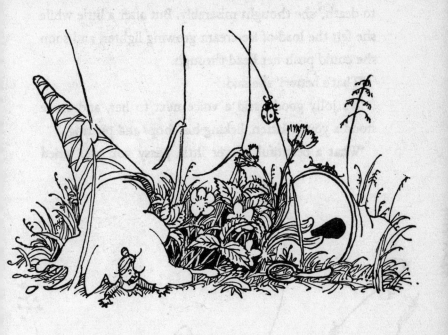

her legs, and then, suddenly, she had SHRUNK to the size of a pepperpot!

There she was, right in Mr Pepperpot's path; she was so afraid he might step on her that she hissed like a snake, and the next thing she knew, she was struggling to get her head clear of a freezing cold and sticky mess! She had only just started breathing again when dollop! She was covered with another portion of ice-cream as big, cold and sticky as the first!

Poor Mrs Pepperpot didn't know what to do; she'd never be able to dig her way out alone. 'I'll just freeze to death,' she thought miserably. But after a little while she felt the load of ice-cream growing lighter, and soon she could push her head through.

'That's better!' she said.

'It's jolly good!' said a voice next to her, and there stood a young kitten, licking his chops and purring.

'What a beautiful, clever little pussy you are!' cried

Mrs Pepperpot, wiping the ice-cream from her face.

'Mm, can't say *you're* exactly beautiful, but you taste very good,' said the kitten. 'Are you made of ice-cream right through? I mean, will I be able to eat you all up?'

'Certainly not!' cried Mrs Pepperpot. 'Ice-cream right through indeed! What an idea! No, my friend, I'm just an ordinary woman most of the time. But now and then I shrink to this size. Come to think of it, I don't mind if you do lick me clean—help yourself!'

The kitten set to work very willingly. He was so thorough that soon Mrs Pepperpot had to shout to him to stop.

'I'm very ticklish, you see,' she said, laughing. 'Fancy me getting a cat-lick; I never expected that when we set off in the car this morning.'

'You have a car?' asked the kitten.

'My husband does; we're on an outing—or we were till this happened. Where do you live?'

The kitten hung his head: 'Nowhere, really. I did live in a barn with my mother, but some people came along and picked me up. They took me back to their house and gave me lots of food—that's where I got my taste for ice-cream. They used to play with me and at night they would tuck me up in a little basket. It was a wonderful life!'

'What happened then?'

'Well, they didn't belong in this place—they were just on holiday. So suddenly, yesterday, they packed up all their stuff, locked the door of the house and got in their car and drove off. I thought I was going too, of course, but they must have forgotten all about me, because they didn't even bother to look back or wave goodbye.'

'I see,' said Mrs Pepperpot, looking thoughtful. 'So now you have no home?'

'No,' said the kitten, 'there's no one to feed me or play with me or call me in at night. Until I found you and the ice-cream I hadn't had anything to eat since yesterday.' He licked the last bit of ice-cream out of Mrs Pepperpot's ear with the point of his rough tongue.

'It was just as well I did shrink today,' said Mrs Pepperpot. 'People like that shouldn't be allowed to keep pets.

Animals are not just playthings for children to throw away when they don't need them any more. Fancy going off and not even asking a neighbour to look after you!' Mrs Pepperpot was getting really worked up, as she always did when people were thoughtless or unkind to animals.

The kitten was watching her with his head on one side: 'Couldn't you take me home with you and let me be your pussy? You're fond of animals, aren't you? And you can talk cat language.'

'Well,' said Mrs Pepperpot, 'there are one or two snags. My husband is *not* very fond of animals, especially young kittens. And as to understanding cat language, I can only do that when I am small.'

'Will you grow large again soon?'

'I don't know.'

'Will I be afraid of you when you do?'

Mrs Pepperpot laughed. 'I shouldn't think so. But if you could manage to carry me on your back over to that old car there, I might grow to my normal size quite soon.'

'I'll try. Climb up!'

But though Mrs Pepperpot got on his back all right, she was too heavy for the kitten to carry.

'Perhaps I could pull you along by your skirt,' he suggested.

'I don't mind what you do,' said Mrs Pepperpot, as she lay down on the ground with her arms tucked under her head; 'pull away!'

The kitten took Mrs Pepperpot's skirt between his teeth and dragged her as carefully as he could down the path, trying to avoid the ice-cream puddle and empty cartons and drinking straws that people had dropped.

'I hope I'm not bumping you too much,' said the kitten.

'Not at all,' answered Mrs Pepperpot, 'I have a fine view of the sky overhead and the birds and the trees.'

But now we had better see what was happening to Mr Pepperpot. We left him in the queue and he stood there a long, long time before he got served again. This time he bought the biggest possible cornet and made

straight for the car, hoping Mrs Pepperpot had not lost patience with him altogether.

'Supposing she has shrunk and I won't be able to find her?' he thought anxiously, but when he opened the back door of the car, there she sat, as large as life.

'Oh my! Am I glad to see you!' He sighed with relief.

'You sound as if I'd been to the moon and back,' she said.

'Well, you see, if you had shrunk and disappeared, I'd never have got through all this ice-cream.' And he held out the cornet.

'Get along with you—I told you to stop fussing,' said Mrs Pepperpot. She set the cornet carefully into the corner of the basket.

'Aren't you going to eat it after all that?' Mr Pepperpot sounded a little hurt.

'All in good time. We'd better be getting on now, if you're going to enter for the rally.'

'I'm not sure I'll bother with that car rally,' he said. 'While I was standing in the queue at the kiosk I heard someone talking about a cross-country race, and it's not as far to drive as the car rally. Shall we go there instead?'

'It's all one to me,' said Mrs Pepperpot, 'as long as we're enjoying ourselves.'

Mr Pepperpot beamed. 'Yes, we are, aren't we?'

He didn't know that Mrs Pepperpot meant herself and the kitten, which was safely hidden in the basket and enjoying a good lick at that giant ice-cream.

II

The road was smooth and they were driving along quite comfortably when Mr Pepperpot suddenly stopped the car.

'Did you hear something?' he asked his wife.

She shook her head. They drove on a bit further, but then he stopped again.

'Didn't you hear anything this time?' he asked.

No, she didn't and he drove on again. But when he stopped for the third time Mr Pepperpot said: 'You must have heard it; it sounded just like a cat miaowing.'

'Probably your brakes have got wet,' suggested Mrs Pepperpot.

'I'll have a look,' said Mr Pepperpot, and got out.

Mrs Pepperpot stayed where she was and stroked the kitten to keep him quiet. After a while she asked her husband if he'd found anything; she knew you shouldn't rush a man when he's looking for trouble in his car.

'Not yet!' came the answer from under the bonnet.

'Perhaps the engine is overheated?'

'Yes, I think I'll get some water from that farm up on the hill.' He took out a green plastic bucket and started trudging up the hill. He could see there was a pump in the front yard.

The farm was quite a long way off, so Mrs Pepperpot thought she could safely take a short stroll with the kitten. The little creature was very good, running along

beside her, purring and rubbing against her skirt.

'You have a better purr than the car engine,' said Mrs Pepperpot. 'Oh, look! There's a pigsty. Let's go and visit the pigs.'

Basking in the sunshine lay a big sow with a whole row of little piglets stretched out beside her. From time to time they woke up, pushed and nudged and sucked and squealed, then they fell asleep again.

Just as she was bending over to stroke the sow, lo and behold! Mrs Pepperpot SHRANK for the second time that day! This was most unusual and quite unexpected.

Luckily, she didn't land among the pigs, but tumbled into a patch of weeds right by the sty.

'Did you hurt yourself? asked a squeaky little voice.

'No, I don't think so, thanks,' said Mrs Pepperpot, struggling to her feet. 'I'm so used to falling—it's almost second nature to me. Hullo! I thought I was talking to a kitten; now I see you're a pig!'

It was indeed a pig, but a very, very small and thin one.

'Don't you belong in there with the others?' asked Mrs Pepperpot.

'I do really. But the farmer put me out. He said my mother had enough to feed and I would have to fend for myself, unless . . .' the piglet put his head on one side and looked wistfully at Mrs Pepperpot from under his white eyelashes, '. . . unless some nice person would take me home and feed me with a bottle.'

'Poor little mite! Does *nobody* want you?'

'Not so far. They all come and look at my mother and the others, gobbling away. But when they see me they just shake their heads and go away,' said the little pig.

'They're stupid and unkind!' said Mrs Pepperpot, 'leaving a fine little fellow like you to starve. I wish I had a bottle of milk handy. If I were my proper size, I'd take you home with me.'

Here the kitten, who had been watching, chipped in: 'You see, Piggy, Mrs Pepperpot isn't always this size—a little while ago she was enormous!'

Mrs Pepperpot laughed. 'I may seem enormous to you, Kitty, but most people call me a *little* old woman. However, what we want right now is to get ourselves over to the farmer's pump. Then, when I grow large again, I can ask if I can have you. My husband's up there too, getting water for his car. But it's too far for me to walk as I am now.'

'I don't think I could carry you,' said the piglet, 'my legs are too wobbly and weak!'

'I'll do what I did before,' said the kitten, 'pull you along by your skirt.'

'Champion!' said Mrs Pepperpot. 'You wait here for us, Piggy. We may be some time, but we'll be back.'

They set off as before, the kitten tugging and pulling Mrs Pepperpot, bumping over the grass and stones. It was hard work up the hill, but the kitten didn't give up till they had reached the pump, where they found the green plastic bucket, but no Mr Pepperpot. He had gone inside to chat with the farmer about the wonders of his old car. They got so interested that when he came out he had forgotten what he came for—to fill his bucket with water.

Mrs Pepperpot, who had hidden inside the bucket when Mr Pepperpot and the farmer came out of the house, wondered if she was going to be left behind. But half-way down the hill Mr Pepperpot remembered the bucket and came rushing back again. The farmer was still standing there: 'You won't get far without water!' he said, as Mr Pepperpot hitched the bucket under the

pump and started pumping.

Poor Mrs Pepperpot! It wasn't very clever of her to hide in the bucket, was it? Now she was in great danger of drowning while Mr Pepperpot went on pumping and talking to the farmer at the same time.

'Travel broadens the mind,' he was saying. 'You need to get out and see for yourself what a beautiful country we live in. D'you know, when I sit behind that wheel with a long clear road in front of me, it often makes me want to sing and shout . . . Ouch!' And he gave a great shout and jumped in the air!

The farmer thought he was showing him what he did when he was driving, but Mr Pepperpot went on jumping about, the bucket fell off the hook and all the water ran out. And Mrs Pepperpot? Well, she had cleverly climbed out of the bucket and had managed to get a hold on Mr Pepperpot's trouser-leg. Then, while he was still talking, she hoisted herself up as far as his braces, but there her foot slipped and she gave him a kick. She also pinched him while trying to stop herself from falling. So that was why Mr Pepperpot shouted: he thought there was an ant inside his shirt.

By now all the rest of the family had come out of the house to look at this funny man dancing round their pump. When he saw they were laughing at him, he ran down the hill to find Mrs Pepperpot and get her to remove the ant, or whatever it was.

But there was no sign of Mrs Pepperpot either in the car or up and down the road.

'Oh dear, oh dear! Now she's shrunk and vanished completely. What shall I do?' After he had hunted around

and called her in vain he suddenly remembered the ant. Heavens! That might have been her! He felt himself all over, but there was no sign of any creepy-crawly now. He would have to go back to the pump. Perhaps he could ask the farmer if he had seen his wife. But how was he going to explain that she might be as small as a tiny doll?

When he got to the pump the whole family was still standing there, so he laughed a little nervously and said: 'I came back for my bucket of water.'

They watched him pump it full again. Then he said: 'Oh, by the way, did you see if I dropped a small doll with a striped skirt on?'

'Doll?' said the farmer. 'No, I didn't see any doll. But I'll ask my wife. Have you seen the gentleman's doll, Kristina?'

'No,' said his wife, 'I didn't see any doll. But I'll ask my daughter. She turned to the eldest girl: 'Have you seen a little doll, Gerda?'

'No,' said Gerda, 'I didn't see any doll. But I'll ask my younger sister, Britta. Did you see a little doll?'

'No,' said Britta, 'but I'll ask my smaller sister, Ada. Did you see a little doll?'

'No,' said Ada, 'but I'll ask my baby sister, Maggie. Did you see a little doll?'

'No,' said Maggie, 'but I'll ask my big brother, Jack. Did you see a little doll?'

'No,' said Jack, 'but I'll ask my bad brother, Ben. Did you see a little doll?'

'No,' said Ben, 'but I'll ask my good brother, Jim. Did you see a little doll?'

'No,' said Jim, 'but I'll ask my sad brother, Frank. Did you see a little doll?'

'No,' said Frank, 'but I'll ask my happy brother, Pete. Did you see a little doll?'

'No,' said Peter, 'but I'll ask my baby brother, John. Did you see a little doll?'

'No,' said Baby John. 'No lil dolly at all!"

'I'm afraid we haven't seen your doll,' said the farmer.

Meanwhile Mr Pepperpot was wringing his hands and muttering to himself: 'I've lost her—this time I really have lost my own dear wife!'

'Did you say *wife*?' asked the farmer with surprise. 'I thought it was a doll you had lost.'

'Well, you see . . . the doll . . . er . . .' Mr Pepperpot didn't know what to say.

'If it's your *wife* you're looking for,' said the farmer, slapping Mr Pepperpot on the back, 'don't worry! We

saw a little old lady in a striped skirt get into your car while you were on your way back here, didn't we, Kristina?'

'Yes,' said his wife, 'and my daughter saw her too, didn't you, Gerda?'

But before the whole family could go through their rigmarole again, Mr Pepperpot was off down the hill, not forgetting the green plastic bucket of water! When he got to the car, there sat Mrs Pepperpot, patiently waiting on the back seat, with her picnic basket on her knee.

Mr Pepperpot was so relieved, he gave her a big kiss. But he couldn't help asking her: 'Did you . . . did you SHRINK?'

'I don't know why you have to keep asking me about

that, Mr P,' said Mrs Pepperpot crossly. 'Try and get that car going for a change!'

This time the car gave no trouble at all, of course. But Mr Pepperpot still felt it would be best to have it checked at the next garage, and Mrs Pepperpot didn't argue, as she wanted to go into the shop right beside it. There she bought a baby's bottle and teat and a pint of milk.

'What do you want that for?' asked her husband when she came back to the car.

'Questions! Questions! When are we going to get to that cross-country race you're so keen to go in for?'

'As a matter of fact, I don't think I *am* so keen now. The man here at the garage has just told me about a fair near

here where they have one of those "trials of strength".
You know; you hit an iron plate with a big hammer as
hard as you can and a disc shoots up to ring a bell. I think
I'd like to have a bash at that. You'd like to go to a fair,
wouldn't you?'

'I expect so. I might try winning something myself,'
said Mrs Pepperpot.

So off they went again: Mr Pepperpot, Mrs Pepperpot,
one kitten and one piglet, which, up to now, had kept
very quiet.

III

They drove on for a while. Mr Pepperpot kept looking out for posters to show where the fair was being held. In the back seat Mrs Pepperpot had made up a little song to keep them amused. This is how it went:

'I know a little pussy-kitten,
   With shiny coat and snowy mitten,
   His ice-cream whiskers wrapped in a rug,
   He's safe inside my basket snug.'

'I like to hear you sing,' said Mr Pepperpot, 'it shows you're feeling happy. I know the tune, too, but I don't remember those words.'

'You're not likely to; I just made them up!' she answered. 'I'll sing you another verse.'

> 'I know a little piggy pink,
> With curly tail and eyes that twink,
> His legs are shaky, but no one mocks,
> He likes to sit in my old box.'

'It's a funny song, all right, and you're a funny old woman,' said Mr Pepperpot.

'Funny yourself!' said his wife. 'Now I'll sing one about you. Here goes:'

> 'I know a man who's not a giant,
> But very smart and self-reliant.
> In motoring he'd spend his life,
> He only fears to lose his wife!'

'There!' shouted Mr Pepperpot, slowing down.

'Where? What?' Mrs Pepperpot didn't know what he was talking about.

'There's the fair. Now I can swing the Big Hammer— you'll see; I'll knock that thingummy right to the top— Ping! Let's see,' he got out and read the poster; 'there are lots of other attractions too; sword-swallowers and tight-rope walkers. . . .'

'I'd be careful about swallowing swords, if I were you,' said Mrs Pepperpot, getting out of the car and closing the door to keep her pets in. 'You make enough fuss if you get as much as a herring-bone in your throat!'

'Silly! They're professionals! Well, I'm going this way to the Big Hammer. Why don't you go and look at the circus animals? They say they're as clever as people.' And with that Mr Pepperpot hurried off into the crowd.

The noise was terrific: hurdy-gurdy music from the merry-go-rounds, people screaming on the Big Wheel, Dodgems clanging and the stall-holders all trying to shout each other down.

Mrs Pepperpot felt quite lost, and wondered where she should go. She decided to buy another ice-cream for the kitten and a carton of milk for that hungry piglet. He had been sleeping quietly in his box since she gave him the first bottle, but soon he'd be awake again, and then he might squeal and give the game away.

Just as she reached the kiosk, Mrs Pepperpot felt the ominous signs—'Not again!' was all she had time to say before she shrank and found herself rolling on the ground with huge boots and shoes tramping all around her.

Was she scared! There was danger from every direction, and she was at her wit's end. Should she try to climb up someone's trouser-leg! Before she could make a grab, however, she found herself picked up by her skirt and whisked away from the tramping feet. Whatever it was, it ran so fast that poor Mrs Pepperpot was slung from side to side and completely lost her breath. She tried to shout 'Let me go!', but then she realised it would be better to let herself get carried out of harm's way. Finally, behind a big tent, whatever-it-was stopped and she felt herself lowered carefully on to the grass. Looking up, she saw, standing over her, a furry creature with black, floppy ears and a big moustache.

'Hullo,' she said. 'What are you supposed to be?'

'Oh,' said the creature, 'I'm just me!'

Mrs Pepperpot laughed. 'I see! I ought to have known. Of course, you're a puppy. Perhaps you're one of those clever circus dogs trained to do tricks?'

'No one's going to train me to do tricks!' declared the puppy, shaking his floppy ears vigorously. 'I do what I want and that's that!'

'Quite right,' said Mrs Pepperpot. 'I do what *I* want, too, except when I turn small like I am now. Then I have

to rely on other people's help. If you can help me now, perhaps *I* can help *you* when I grow large. But I can only understand animal language when I am small, so if you've anything to tell me, you'd better do it now.'

Then the puppy told her his story in little excited barks. He really belonged to the circus manager, but when he wouldn't learn to count and to bark in the key of F major, the manager chased him out of his tent.

'But you haven't heard the worst,' added the puppy.

'Let's have it,' said Mrs Pepperpot.

The puppy put his head on one side and looked at her sadly. 'Are you pedigree?' he asked.

'Well,' laughed Mrs Pepperpot, 'I've never really thought about it. I don't think I care if I am or not.'

'As a dog, if you're not pedigree, you're useless, that's what they told me,' said the puppy.

'Never mind! You have a beautiful moustache.'

'They said it didn't belong with my kind of breed.'

'Bother them and their pedigree!' said Mrs Pepperpot.
'That moustache will come in very handy, for you and I
are going to fool the whole lot of them!'

The puppy looked at her with big round eyes. 'Why,
what are we going to do?'

'You must pick me up very carefully in your mouth,
just like you did before,' said Mrs Pepperpot. 'And now
jump straight on to the roof of that caravan!'

It was a most tremendous leap, but the puppy arrived
safely with Mrs Pepperpot in his mouth. Then Mrs
Pepperpot draped his long moustache over her skirts
and legs, so that she was completely hidden. At first no

one noticed them up there, but when the music stopped for a pause Mrs Pepperpot suddenly started to sing through the puppy's moustache:

'Baa, baa, black sheep,
Here we go gathering nuts in May,
Who killed Cock Robin?
Three blind mice, three blind mice,
Little Tommy Tucker,
Sing a song of sixpence,
Girls and boys come out to play,
See saw, Marjorie Daw.'

Wasn't that an old jumble of a song? But it was the best she could do, hanging there in mid-air. The people standing round the caravan were astonished to see a puppy on the roof, and even more amazed that he was singing. Others joined them to watch; the roundabout came to a halt, the passengers left the Dodgems, and even the circus performance stopped as the audience flocked outside to hear the clever puppy sing.

The circus manager himself appeared. 'Hi!' he shouted, 'that's my puppy! Here, boy; here, boy!' But the puppy took no notice; it was all he could do to keep his balance with Mrs Pepperpot in his mouth.

'Can you count to ten?' shouted the circus manager. 'One?' No answer. 'Two?' Silence. 'Three? Four? Five?' Still no answer from the puppy. 'You're just having us on, you obstinate little brute! Six, seven, eight, nine, ten . . .'

Mrs Pepperpot decided it was time to teach the circus manager a lesson. In a high, yappy voice she said quickly: 'Eleven, twelve, thirteen, fourteen, fifteen, sixteen, seventeen, eighteen, nineteen, twenty!'

Consternation in the crowd! The circus manager jumped up and down, whooping with excitement. There was such a crush of people trying to see the puppy that they overturned the caravan and everyone fell on top of everyone else! When at last they had sorted themselves out, the puppy had disappeared. He and Mrs Pepperpot had jumped clear when the caravan toppled, and had made for the car as fast as his little legs could carry them.

When Mr Pepperpot returned, his wife, who was now

her proper size, was wrapping something up in an old coat they kept in the back of the car.

Mr Pepperpot was so excited about the singing puppy, he didn't notice what she was doing. 'You should have heard him—he sang a whole song!'

Mrs Pepperpot laughed. 'Get along with you! A dog singing!'

'I saw him with my own eyes!' he assured her. Then he looked thoughtful for a moment and said: 'Come to think of it, it was rather like one of your daft songs!'

'Was it, indeed?' Mrs Pepperpot looked pained. 'How did you get on with the Big Hammer?'

'With all that fuss about the puppy, I didn't get time to try it. Anyway, I heard someone talking about a walking contest. So I thought I'd drive a little further and try that.'

'Very well,' said Mrs Pepperpot with a sigh. She was beginning to wonder if they'd ever get home that day;

if they had to stay overnight somewhere, what would she do with the animals?

But Mr Pepperpot drove happily on, and in the back seat—though he didn't know it—he now had *four* passengers: Mrs Pepperpot, the kitten, the piglet and the puppy with black floppy ears and a big moustache.

IV

When they had driven another few miles Mr Pepperpot stopped the car.

'I don't know what's wrong,' he said, 'but the car seems so heavy at the back. Perhaps the tyres are going flat; I expect I'd better pump them up a bit. You'll have to get out meanwhile.'

Mrs Pepperpot didn't like this idea. If her husband started rummaging in the back of the car he might find the animals.

'I don't feel like getting out just now,' she said. 'Can't it wait till you get to the next petrol station? Then they can do it for you.'

'I suppose so,' he said and drove on. But soon he was grumbling again: 'Why can't you sit still? If there's not

enough room for you in the back seat, you could throw out some of that food.'

He didn't know that the food had been eaten up long ago by the piglet, the kitten and the puppy.

'If anything's to be thrown out, it's not the food!' said Mrs Pepperpot quite huffily. 'If your old car can't even carry one passenger, Mr P, *I* can get out, and you can go on alone!'

This was very cunning of Mrs Pepperpot, because if there is one thing a proud car-owner hates, it is criticism of his beautiful automobile.

'You stay right where you are!' said Mr Pepperpot. 'It's not really the weight that matters, but all the strange noises I have been hearing from the back. I must find out what's causing them.'

'Oh dear!' sighed Mrs Pepperpot, 'that must have been my singing you could hear. I was making up a sort of song—not a proper one, you understand, for *I* have never sung in a choir like *you* . . .'

Mr Pepperpot brightened up at the word 'choir', as he had been very good at choir-singing when he was young.

'That's right, my dear,' he said, 'not everyone is born with a beautiful voice. But you go right ahead and sing; nothing like it for uplifting the soul and making us think of the joys of spring!'

'Don't know so much about the joys of spring,' muttered Mrs Pepperpot, 'it's more like a farmyard when I get going. But you asked for it:

> 'Dogs are lots of fun,
> When they jump and run,
> But when they start to yap-yap,
> They will get a slap-slap!
>
> Cats are sweet and furry,
> Never in a hurry
> Till they start a row-row,
> Fight and scratch and miaow-miaow!
>
> As for little pigs,
> See them dancing jigs;
> Their little feet go boink-boink
> While their snouts go oink-oink!'

'Ridiculous!' was Mr Pepperpot's comment. 'This time I didn't even know the tune.'

'Nor did I when I started,' said Mrs Pepperpot. 'I can see a petrol station over there.'

'Good,' said Mr Pepperpot. He stopped at the garage and asked the man to pump up his tyres, and Mrs Pepperpot hoped the animals would keep quiet meanwhile. But she needn't have worried, for her husband was soon deep in conversation with the the garage man about a fishing competition which was due to start at two o'clock.

'You can put your name on this list,' the man was

saying, 'and then I'll show you which way to go.'

Mr Pepperpot signed his name to show he was a competitor, and they set off again, this time down a narrow lane through a wood. It was lovely and cool in there and soon they got to a little green glade.

'This is where the man said I could park the car,' said Mr Pepperpot. He got out and fetched his fishing tackle from the boot. 'I suppose you don't want to come and watch me?'

'I'd rather wait for you to bring me back a lovely fish for my supper. I'll just lie in the nice grass and watch the trees for a bit.'

'Bye, bye, then,' said Mr Pepperpot, walking off towards the river, hopeful as ever.

Mrs Pepperpot called 'Good luck!' after him, but as soon as he was out of sight she opened the basket to let the kitten and the piglet out and unrolled the puppy, who had been having a nice nap inside the old coat. They all came tumbling out on the grass. At first the

kitten was a bit frightened and arched his back and hissed at the puppy, but soon they were all three chasing each other round and round. Mrs Pepperpot sat on a tree-stump in the middle and enjoyed the fun. When she thought they had had enough exercise she caught them all and put them back in the car.

'Be good,' she told them. 'I'm going to the shop on the main road to buy some more food for you.' And she shut the car door securely.

It was very pleasant walking along the quiet lane, and

she was quite sorry to get back on to the dusty road. Luckily, the shop wasn't far. It was one of those old-fashioned country stores where they sell everything from pickled herrings in barrels to hair-nets, barbed wire and liquorice. When she got there a lot of people were waiting to be served, so she took a stroll round the back where she found a chicken-yard. She counted twelve

fine hens, pecking and scraping in the sand, but over in a corner stood a miserable little bird, blinking her eyes and shivering. She looked so bedraggled and thin that Mrs Pepperpot at once felt sorry for her.

'You poor thing! But don't you worry; I'll have you out of here in no time, as sure as my name's Pepperpot!'

The little hen didn't seem to hear her, but Mrs Pepperpot went back inside and bought her provisions. When she had finished she asked the little man behind the counter if he would sell her the hen.

'Oh, you don't want that miserable creature!' he exclaimed. 'She's never been any good at laying eggs, and now she's getting old and tough too.'

'We none of us get any younger,' said Mrs Pepperpot, 'and she hasn't had much of a chance, being chased round the yard from morning till night.' As you know, when Mrs Pepperpot makes up her mind she can be very determined, and at last the little man gave in. He found a big cardboard box and put the hen in it. She was so scared she lay absolutely still.

Mrs Pepperpot left the shop with the cardboard box under one arm and the basket of food under the other. It was quite a heavy load for her to carry, and when she reached the lane she put both down, so that she could

change hands and have a rest. Also she wanted to see if the hen was all right. She lifted the lid just a little.

'Mercy!' she shouted, for at that moment she SHRANK for the *fourth* time that day and toppled in with the hen!

More frightened than ever, the bird flapped out of the box, but Mrs Pepperpot managed to cling on to one of her legs. This stopped the hen from flying away.

'Woah!' said Mrs Pepperpot. 'Stand still while I get on your back.' The hen was squawking, and as soon as Mrs Pepperpot was on her back she ran as fast as she could into the bushes, where she got stuck.

'You're a scatter-brain and no mistake!' Mrs Pepperpot told her when they were out in the lane again.

'That's what they've all said—ever since I was born,' said the hen sadly.

Mrs Pepperpot patted her neck. 'I'm sorry, I didn't mean to hurt your feelings. Don't you bother what people say. From now on you're coming to live with me and be my very special feathered friend.'

'Thanks very much, but would you tell me where we are going and how we are going to get anywhere with you such a very small person?'

'Quite right, I should have said. I want you to take me along this lane till we get to my husband's car. I'm not this size all the time, you see, and should be back to normal human size soon.'

'Well, I hope you hurry up, because I can see the fox over there in the bushes!' said the hen, blinking her eyes nervously in that direction. Sure enough! There stood Master Fox, and he was licking his chops.

'Don't worry,' whispered Mrs Pepperpot, 'I'll deal with him!' Out loud she said: 'I see a certain well-known person is out for a walk in the sunshine.'

'That's right. I was giving myself an appetite for my dinner. And I seem to be in luck,' laughed the fox, 'as my dinner is out walking too!' And he made ready to spring on the hen.

'Hold on!' shouted Mrs Pepperpot. 'Don't be in too much of a hurry, Master Fox. You see, I'm going round with invitations to a picnic, so I may as well invite you too. That is, if you'll behave like a gentleman.'

'Very funny!' said the fox, showing his teeth. 'Of course you thought you could trick me like the cockerel once did when he got me to wash my paws before I started eating. I know that one!' He put one paw on the hen, who was trembling all over by now.

But Mrs Pepperpot kept calm. 'I'm not trying to trick you,' she said. 'If you'll let go of the hen at once I promise you'll have a meal much better than a tough old bird. But first I want you to carry the basket of groceries over to that car in the glade. Then you can come back and fetch me and the hen.'

'Oh no!' cackled the hen, more terrified than ever.

'Another trick!' said the fox. 'When I get back you'll both be gone. I want my food *now*!' He put the other paw on Mrs Pepperpot's skirt.

'How stupid you are!' said Mrs Pepperpot. 'I've always heard that foxes were so smart, but that must have been in the old days. If you're afraid of losing us, the hen can carry me on her back and we'll walk beside you all the way.'

The fox agreed. He took the basket in his mouth and the hen carried Mrs Pepperpot on her back till they reached the car. Once there, Mrs Pepperpot asked the fox to unpack the food and sent the hen up on the roof of the car to fetch a plastic tablecloth which they spread on the grass.

'When do we start the feast?' asked the fox.

'We'll have to wait till I collect the rest of the guests,' said Mrs Pepperpot. Then she put her hand to her mouth and shouted with all her might: 'Are you there, Great Cat Tiger-claws?'

'Miaow!' said a little voice from the car.

'What's this?' demanded the fox. 'Are there other guests invited?'

'Oh yes!' answered Mrs Pepperpot, putting her hand to her mouth again. 'Are you there, Wild Boar Gory

Fangs?' she shouted as loudly as she could.

'Oink! Oink!' came the reply from the car.

'Good heavens! Are there any more?' The fox was beginning to look nervous.

'Wait and see!' said Mrs Pepperpot. 'Are you there, Handlebar Moustachio Foxhunter?'

'Woof! Woof!' answered the puppy.

'Thanks very much' said the fox. 'I don't think I fancy this picnic after all!'

'Oh, come on! They'll all be very pleased to see you,' said Mrs Pepperpot. 'You just sit down and enjoy yourself. The hen can sit next to you if you like.'

'I'd rather not!' said the poor hen, who didn't trust the fox one inch.

The fox looked hurt. 'You've tricked me just like the others,' he said. But Mrs Pepperpot shook her head:

'No. I promised you food, and I keep my promises. You can put a large chunk of ham and some fresh eggs in the basket and take it away to eat. Will that satisfy you?'

'Very generous, I'm sure,' said the fox, collecting the food in the basket and picking it up.

Just as he was about to run off with it, Mrs Pepperpot said: 'Just a minute! One thing more. I want the basket back.'

'All right,' said the fox, 'if you can keep your promises,

I can keep mine. I'll see you get it back.' With that he
vanished in the bushes, much to the hen's relief.

At that moment Mrs Pepperpot grew to her proper
size. She lost no time in getting her pets out and they all
had a lovely picnic in the grass. She had just finished
putting them back in their different hiding places when
Mr Pepperpot returned from his fishing contest. But
she could see from his face that there would be no fish
for supper *that* night.

'What happened?' she asked.

'Oh,' he said despondently, 'it wasn't much of a turn-
out. We had an hour for the contest, but I never got a
single bite. And then something very strange happened.'

'What was that?'

'Well, you see this basket?' He held up a basket still wet.
'D'you recognise it?'

'It's our picnic basket,' she said.

'That's right! What I want to know is: how did it come to be floating downstream towards me when you are here, much further down the river?' Mr Pepperpot was scratching his head and looking very puzzled.

Mrs Pepperpot could hardly stop herself from laughing, but she just said: 'I have no idea! How did you get it back?'

'It floated straight on to my line, so I hooked it out.'

'Life's full of surprises, isn't it?' said Mrs Pepperpot, getting back in the car. 'Now let's get on, Mr P, or we'll never get home today.'

So Mr Pepperpot turned the car out of the little glade and drove off with Mrs Pepperpot, the kitten, the piglet, the puppy and the hen all on the back seat.

V

They had not gone many miles when Mr Pepperpot put his foot on the brake and stopped very sharply.

'*Now* what's up?' asked Mrs Pepperpot, who had been having a little doze.

'There's a poster about a contest,' said Mr Pepperpot. 'I want to see what it says.'

'Don't you think we've had enough contests for today? We're getting tired and it's time to go home.'

'Speak for yourself, Mrs P.—I'm not tired,' said Mr Pepperpot.

'Anyway, I wish you wouldn't put the brakes on so suddenly, you should think of us in the back seat,' said Mrs Pepperpot.

'Us? Who's us?' he asked.

'Why . . . er . . . the baggage and me!' Mrs Pepperpot was a little flustered—she had nearly given the game away! But her husband had now got out of the car to look at the poster, and this is what it said:

SENSATIONAL SPORTS EVENT TODAY
The Great Traditional Cross-Country Race
starting from Railway Square at 4 p.m.

The Course is as Follows:
Cross Bilberry Marsh by mapped-out Route,
Wade over Black River above the Waterfall,
Take 12 ft Leap from Red Cliff on the North bank
to White Rock on the South bank. Run to
finishing line at the Big Spruce Tree.
1st Prize a Silver Cup.
Refreshments Served.

'Mercy me!' said Mrs Pepperpot when her husband read it out. 'You're never thinking of entering that one, are you?'

'Well, I don't know,' he said. 'I'd like to watch it anyway.'

'And what are we going to do meanwhile?' she asked.

Mr Pepperpot stared at her. 'You said "we" again!'

'Oh well!' she said crossly, 'you keep stopping and starting, and messing about—is it any wonder if I get mixed up? What am *I* going to do, then? Sit in this stuffy old car?'

'No. As you say you're tired, I'll drop you at the station and you take the train home.'

Mrs Pepperpot thought this over, but then she agreed. 'As long as you leave the car in the station yard and promise me not to take part in the stupid competition,' she said.

He promised and drove the car to the station, where he parked it. He gave Mrs Pepperpot some money to get home and then he went round the other side to the Railway Square to watch the competitors line up for the race.

When he was out of sight Mrs Pepperpot went over to the ticket office. There she bought a ticket for herself and paid for the animals to be put in a wooden crate, so that they could travel in the guard's van. A nice guard helped her get the animals in.

'I'll stay with them till the train comes,' she told the guard, and sat down on the crate. But just as the train pulled up at the platform poor Mrs Pepperpot did her fifth SHRINKING for that day! The crate had wide gaps between the boards, and Mrs Pepperpot fell straight through on to the kitten's tail!

'Miaow!' said the kitten, 'that hurt!'

'Sssh! Don't make a noise,' said Mrs Pepperpot, 'just try and hide me—I don't want the guard to see me like this!'

The animals did their best: the kitten curled his tail over her dress, the puppy spread one ear over her blouse and the hen held one wing carefully over her face. The pig just stretched out beside her and blinked at her from under his white eyelashes. When the guard came back he lifted the crate into the guard's van. Then he looked round for the old woman. Where could she have gone? It was only a little train, so he looked into all the carriages and asked the station-master if he had seen her. She was nowhere.

But the train couldn't wait, so the guard blew his whistle and off they went. The animals were delighted to have Mrs Pepperpot with them. 'How lucky you shrank just now!' they said.

'Well, you'd better make the most of me while you have me,' she told them. 'After five shrinkings in one day I don't suppose it will happen again for a long time. So, if you have any questions, fire away!'

The animals all lined up like a row of school-children with Mrs Pepperpot as their very small teacher standing out in front.

The kitten began: 'Please, ma'am, when do we get to your house?'

'In time for supper,' said Mrs Pepperpot firmly, but to herself she added 'I hope', for she wondered what would happen when they got to their station.

'What am I going to have to eat?' asked the piglet.

'Don't worry, there's a whole bin of lovely mash for piglets at my house,' she assured him.

'What about dogs?' asked the puppy. 'Can I do as I like?''

'Certainly!' said Mrs Pepperpot. 'Liberty Hall, that's what they call my place!'

The hen looked anxiously at her. 'Will there be a lot of other hens in your yard? Will they peck me?'

'You shall be my one and only special hen; didn't I tell you?' said Mrs Pepperpot.

All the animals clapped and flapped and stamped and shouted: 'Hooray for Mrs Pepperpot!'

To keep them from getting too boisterous and to while away the time she decided to teach them a song. 'Listen

carefully,' she said, 'and come in when I point to you.'
She began to sing.

> 'Children all, now gather round,
> And let us make a jolly sound,
> First a dog and then a cat,
> A little pig, a hen, all pat!
>
> Here we go: sing as I do,
> Puppy dog, a bark from you!
> Woof, woof! Woof, woof!'

Here she pointed to the puppy and he barked as loudly
as he could: 'Woof, woof! Woof, woof!'

> 'Here we go: sing as I do,
> Little Puss, a song from you!
> Miaow, miaow! Miaow, miaow!'

The kitten didn't wait to be asked, but sang in chorus
with Mrs Pepperpot: 'Miaow, miaow! Miaow, miaow!'

> 'Here we go: sing as I do,
> Piglet, we must hear from you!
> Oink, oink! Oink, oink!'

When Mrs Pepperpot pointed at him, the piglet got so
carried away, he wouldn't stop 'oinking', and the puppy
had to give him a sharp nip.

> 'Here we go: sing as I do,
> Hennypen, a cluck from you!
> Cluck, cluck! Cluck, cluck!'

But the hen was so frightened by all the noise the others had made, she only managed a very small 'cluck, cluck!' the first time. However, they went on practising, and by the time the train stopped at their station they were all singing very well indeed.

The guard opened the door and lifted the crate on to a trolley with a lot of milk-churns. As nobody else got out of the train he blew the whistle and it moved off. Luckily Mrs Pepperpot's name and address were written on the lid, so when Peter, the milkman, came in his van to fetch the churns he saw the crate and thought he was meant to deliver it together with the milk. This saved Mrs Pepperpot a lot of trouble, for as soon as he had put the crate down at the corner of the road leading to her house, and had driven off, there was an almighty CRASH!

Mrs Pepperpot grew so fast that she burst right through the crate, scattering the animals and the boards pell-mell all around. Such a to-do! The hen landed on the branch of a tree, the puppy rolled down the hill, the piglet got his snout stuck in a hole and the poor kitten fell in the stream!

When Mrs Pepperpot had picked herself up she quickly collected all the animals. She put the hen under one arm and the piglet under the other and called the kitten and the puppy to follow her. All together they climbed the hill to her house.

'Here we are, children, home at last!' she said, as she opened the door, and set the hen and the piglet down. The kitten and the puppy trotted in after her and now they were all nosing round to see what their new house was like.

Mrs Pepperpot sat down. She had a problem. Mr Pepperpot was bound to come home soon. How was she going to tell him about the additions to their family? She put her finger on her nose and thought. Then she cried: 'I've got it! I have a solution!'

First she put the kitten in the bed and covered him with the counterpane. Then she put the piglet in the empty wood-box by the stove and sprinkled wood-shavings all over him. The puppy she hid in a basket under the table, and the hen she lifted up on the bureau. 'You keep very still,' she told her, 'I'm going to cover you up.' And she put a large lampshade over her. Then she put the coffee on and went outside to see if her husband was coming.

There he was, struggling up the hill, looking so downcast that she had to shout and wave to him to let him know she was there. When he did see her his whole face lit up and he fairly sprinted up the last bit of the road.

'Am I glad you're here!' he said, giving her a big kiss.

'Why shouldn't I be here, Mr P?' said Mrs Pepperpot. 'What have you done with the car?'

'I couldn't very well take it through the bog and jump it over the river, could I?'

Mrs Pepperpot threw up her hands in horror: 'You never went in for that race, did you? After promising...?'

'I know. I only meant to watch it. But then I heard the railway guard asking people if they'd seen a little old woman who was supposed to be travelling on the train to our station. He said she'd disappeared. So, of course, I thought at once it must be you who had turned small.'

'What happened then?' she asked.

'Well, I tried to jump on the train, which was just pulling out, but I couldn't catch it. So I headed straight for Bilberry Marsh. I knew it was a short cut and it would have taken much longer to drive the car round by the road.'

'Go on!' said Mrs Pepperpot, all ears.

'The path across the marsh was clearly marked for the race and it took me straight to the place above the waterfall where you have to wade across. Then I scrambled down the other side till I got to Red Cliff.'

Mrs Pepperpot's eyes were popping out of her head by now: 'You didn't take the twelve-foot leap to White Rock, did you?'

'Of course I did; there was no other way!'

'Then you must have won the race!' said Mrs Pepperpot. 'Did they give you the Prize Cup?'

'I didn't wait for anything like that. All I was thinking about was getting to the station in time to get you out of the train. But I was too late and I thought I'd never see you again.'

'Silly!' said Mrs Pepperpot, but she was wiping her eyes with her apron and sniffing a little. 'Come on in and have some coffee.'

When he was sitting comfortably with his cup of coffee she patted his cheek and said: 'Thanks for the outing. I enjoyed it!'

He smiled. 'I'm glad! And you didn't shrink, did you?'

'Well . . . er . . . actually I did—five times in all.'

'You SHRANK FIVE TIMES???' Mr Pepperpot looked thunderstruck.

Mrs Pepperpot decided to tell him the whole story

'The first time I was very frightened in case you should leave me behind.'

'You know I'd never do that!' said Mr Pepperpot.

She smiled at him. 'No, you wouldn't, would you? Not many people have such kind husbands as *I* have. Well, the first time I shrank I met a kitten. The family he belonged to had gone back to town and left him—just like that—with no food or shelter. Would you have done that?'

'No indeed, that's a terrible thing to do!' said Mr Pepperpot.

'I knew that's how you would feel. So I thought it best to take the kitten along with me. Pussy! Pussy! You can come out now and meet your new master!'

'Miaow!' said the kitten and stuck his little head out from the bedclothes.

'Well, I'll be . . . !' said Mr Pepperpot. But Mrs Pepperpot was already hurrying him back into the kitchen.

'The second time I shrank,' she said, 'I met a piglet. That was when you went to get water from the pump, remember?'

'So it *was* you and not an ant climbing up my trouser-leg?'

'It was. But never mind that. The little pig had been thrown out by the farmer to fend for himself, and he was so miserable I *had* to help him. I mean, *I've* never had to go hungry in my life—have you?'

'Well, no, I suppose I haven't . . .' said Mr Pepperpot, scratching his head.

'There, you see, I knew you would agree. Come on, Piggy, show yourself to Mr Pepperpot!' And out of

the shavings in the wood-box came first a pair of pink ears, then a little pink snout and lastly a whole pink piglet.

'Good gracious!' said Mr Pepperpot.

'But that's not all,' said his wife. 'The third time I shrank was at the fair. There I was, right on the ground under all those people's feet . . .'

Mr Pepperpot was holding his ears. 'Stop! Don't tell me! One of these days you'll get yourself killed.'

'Ah, but I was rescued by a very clever puppy, one that had you all gasping with his singing and his counting.'

'No! You don't mean to say that that was you as well?'

Mrs Pepperpot nodded. 'But I think it's more important that a dog should be a real dog and not learn circus tricks —a dog that can be your friend and protect you.'

'You mean we ought to have a guard dog?' said Mr Pepperpot.

'That's right, and I have the very one. Out you come, Puppy! Show your master how clever you are!'

'Woof! Woof!' barked the puppy excitedly, as he danced round Mr Pepperpot's feet.

'You see, he's your friend already," said Mrs Pepperpot, as her husband bent down to pat the floppy black ears and pull that long moustache.

'Good dog!' he said.

'The fourth time was when you were fishing. I had gone to the shop for some groceries, and I bought a hen because she didn't lay eggs.'

'Because she *didn't* lay eggs?' Mr Pepperpot was getting quite confused.

'Well no, you see, she was being hen-pecked by all the other birds in the yard, so she didn't really have a chance.'

'Cluck-cluck-cluck-alooooh!' The sound came from under the lampshade. Mrs Pepperpot hurried to take it off, and there stood the hen on the bureau, and under her lay a large, brown egg!

Mr Pepperpot burst out laughing: 'She's certainly making up for lost time!'

'She laid it specially for you!' said Mrs Pepperpot, 'because you're the kindest and most understanding of husbands, and all the animals love you!'

'Steady on!' protested Mr Pepperpot. 'You know very well it's you the animals love. You must have the first egg!'

'I don't care what you say, this one's going to be fried for you!' And she cracked it on the edge of the frying-pan while Mr Pepperpot watched. Into the hot fat fell two golden yolks!

'That hen knows how to keep the peace,' said Mr Pepperpot, 'now we can each have an egg!'

When they had had their supper Mrs Pepperpot said: 'I have one more surprise for you.'

Mr Pepperpot groaned: 'Not another animal, I hope.'

'Come into the parlour and I'll show you,' she said and opened the door. There on the table stood a brightly polished silver cup.

'That's for you!' she said. 'You've certainly earned it today.'

'But that's the cup you won for handling livestock when you were a young girl working on the farm!'

'Well, I give it to you now because you're just as good at handling livestock!' answered Mrs Pepperpot.

'I suppose we could hold it jointly . . .?' suggested Mr Pepperpot.

'That's a very good idea. And now, have you thought what you will do with the rest of your holiday?' she asked him.

'I can't say I have, but I don't think I'll do any more motoring.'

'Good!' said Mrs Pepperpot, 'I think it's very nice to stay at home sometimes. And then you can get out your tool-box and build a pen for the piglet, a run for the hen, a kennel for the dog and . . .'

'And *nothing* for the cat!' said Mr Pepperpot firmly. But the kitten didn't mind; he was already stretched out in his favourite spot—along the top of Mr Pepperpot's armchair.

Mrs Pepperpot has a Visitor from America

IT's not so often that there's a letter in the post for Mrs Pepperpot. But one day when she opened her letter-box she found a big letter with many foreign stamps on it. It was from her sister who lives in St. Paul, Minnesota, U.S.A., and this is what it said:

Dear Sister,

I am now on my way to the Old Country and would like to visit you. Can you come and meet me at Fornebu Airport? That will make me very, very happy.

Your loving sister, Margret Anne

'Well, well!' said Mrs Pepperpot to herself, 'so my loving sister is coming back to Norway? It must be forty years since we last saw each other and there wasn't much loving sister about her then. As I remember it, I always got the short end of the stick. We'd go to the store and it would be little me to carry the basket while Miss Hoity Toity Margret Anne talked with the boys. And at school . . . I shall never forget the day she said I'd spilt ink over her copy-book and ruined it. As if I'd do a thing like that! Then there was the other time she fell in the brook and said I'd pushed her in. If we went blueberry picking she'd pinch my basket because it was full and she was too lazy to get her own. And then . . .'

But we won't go on listening to all this miserable stuff, because it's quite clear that Mrs Pepperpot was in a very bad mood that day. All the same, her sister would have to be met at the airport; there was no getting away from that!

'I'll go,' said Mrs Pepperpot, 'but if Margret Anne thinks I'm going to doll myself up for her sake, she's much mistaken! I'll put on some old clothes of our mother's and a shawl round my head, and I'll take my broom along. Then my fine sister may not even want to know me!'

The day came and Mrs Pepperpot took the bus to the airport. It was quite a long trip and the other passengers were a bit surprised to see her get on in her old-fashioned clothes and carrying a broom.

At the airport there was a great crowd of people, and they stared even more at the little old woman with her shawl and her broom. Some of them were talking in foreign languages, and everyone was carrying heavy suitcases and pushing this way and that. By the time the loudspeaker announced that the plane from New York was about to land, Mrs Pepperpot was so confused, she didn't know if she was standing on her head or her heels. As it happened, it didn't matter very much, because at that moment she SHRANK!

'Oh my goodness!' wailed Mrs Pepperpot, as she rolled along the slippery floor and very nearly got trodden on,

'What a time for this to happen!'

But almost at once she felt herself snatched up by a large lady's hand and popped into a glass show-case.

'Somebody must have been trying to steal one of the souvenirs,' said the large lady and locked the door of the show-case.

There stood Mrs Pepperpot, shawl, broom and all! She could see the people coming in from the plane, and among them, looking anxiously round, was a lady in a smart fawn hat and flowers on her coat and dress which matched the flowers on her outsize handbag. She wore spectacles with jewelled rims which sparkled most amazingly.

'That must be Margret Anne,' thought Mrs Pepperpot, and a moment later she was sure, because the lady walked past the show-case talking aloud to herself:

'Oh dear, where can my sister be? I'd better wait a bit.'

She came back and looked into the show-case.

'Maybe I should buy some Norwegian souvenirs for my friends in America. Oh, what a wonderful doll! She looks just like my mother with that shawl, and she used to have a broom just like that. But the face isn't like her—oh no it has such a bad-tempered expression!'

Mrs Pepperpot was fuming inside: 'Has it indeed! I wonder what your mother would say if she could see *you*, dressed up as you are, in your American finery!'

Margret Anne went on talking to herself: 'I really must buy that doll to show my sister; she'll think it very, very funny!'

Mrs Pepperpot didn't think it funny at all, but held herself as stiff as she could while the large lady picked her up and gave her to Margret Anne, who paid for her and put her in her outsize handbag. Before it was closed, Mrs Pepperpot had time to see what a lot of knick-knacks there were inside: powder compact, lipsticks, paper hankies, face-cream, notebooks, pens and pencils, cigarettes. . . . Once the lid was closed Mrs Pepperpot was almost suffocated with all the different smells and she badly wanted to sneeze. But she kept as still as a mouse while her sister called a taxi.

Margret Anne told the taxi-man to drive all the way to the valley where Mrs Pepperpot lived, which was many miles away.

'That'll cost her a pretty penny!' thought Mrs Pepperpot. 'But at least I'll get a free ride.'

The taxi drove on and on, and Mrs Pepperpot must have had a little snooze, because suddenly she woke up to hear her sister say: 'Driver! Stop at this shop, please! I haven't been here since I was a child, and I want to go in and buy a few things for my sister. When she was a little girl she was always so good about carrying the groceries home for me.'

'Well, I never!' said Mrs Pepperpot inside the handbag.

Margret Anne went up to the counter and bought some smoked fish, some goat-milk cheese and some strong Norwegian sausage.

'I haven't tasted these things for forty years,' she told the grocer, who was a young man and didn't remember Margret Anne. She put all the things in her handbag on top of poor Mrs Pepperpot.

'Pooh!' said Mrs Pepperpot. 'I'll die if I have to stay in this smelly bag much longer!'

Just as she was going out of the shop, Margret Anne asked the grocer if he had a small bottle of ink.

'Good gracious! What does she want that for?' thought Mrs Pepperpot, as the ink bottle was poked into a corner beside her.

Then she heard her sister ask the taxi-man to drive to the school-house.

'I want to look at the room where my sister and I learned our lessons. It's all so long ago, but I've often thought how unkind I was when I told the teacher my sister poured ink on my copy-book.'

'I see!' thought Mrs Pepperpot. 'The bottle of ink is a peace-offering. Better late than never!'

When she had looked inside the little old school-room, Margret Anne asked the driver to stop a short way out of the village where there was a bridge over the brook.

'You see, that's where I once fell in when I was a child and I told my mother that my sister pushed me.'

'I got a good hiding for that, my fine lady!' said Mrs Pepperpot inside the bag.

'I'd like to sit on the bridge for a moment and think about how wicked I was. D'you think my sister will have forgiven me?'

The taxi-man laughed: 'Why, ma'am,' he said, 'she'll

be so pleased to see you after all these years, she won't worry about your little tiffs when you were young!'

'Perhaps she's not so bad, after all,' thought Mrs Pepperpot.

Margret Anne was dangling her legs over the edge of the bridge and staring down into the water, when suddenly she saw a great fish swimming by. She got so excited, she dropped the handbag into the brook!

'Help, help!' cried Mrs Pepperpot, as the bag went whirling downstream. She was rolling round and round inside with the cheese and the fish and, worst of all, the ink! The cap had come off and she was covered in the

stuff. Luckily the bag hit a stone which forced the catch open and Mrs Pepperpot was thrown out.

Remembering a diving lesson a frog had given her once, she went in head first to clean off the ink, and then she swam to the bank, pulling the bag after her.

'Now if only I could get back to my proper size!' she said, and, for once, it actually happened as she wished.

She was not far from home, so she ran up the hill as fast as she could go and into her house.

When Margret Anne arrived a few minutes later in the taxi, there stood her sister to greet her at the door, wearing a nice clean frock and with her hair neatly combed.

'Aw, honey! It's good to see my little sister after all

these years!' cried Margret Anne, as she flung her arms round Mrs Pepperpot's neck.

'Little is right,' thought Mrs Pepperpot, but all she said was: 'You're very welcome, Margret Anne, I'm sure.' She could see the taxi-man was grinning as he turned the car down the hill.

'Come on in and make yourself at home!' she went on, and led her sister indoors where the table was laid with strawberry layer-cake and pancakes with blueberry jam.

Margret Anne walked round admiring everything and saying how wonderful it was to be home. Then she remembered the lost handbag.

'It just fell out of my hand,' she told Mrs Pepperpot, 'and the water was running so fast it disappeared before we could catch it, though the driver did his best. I had everything in it, except my money, but what I'm really sorry about, honey, was a little old doll, dressed in a long black skirt with a shawl over its head and carrying a broom. It looked so like our mother—you'd have died laughing!'

'Is this the handbag!' asked Mrs Pepperpot, shyly holding up a large wet object that was still dripping on the floor. 'I got out of it—I mean, I *found* it—just down below the hill. But the doll has gone, I'm afraid.'

'How sad!' said Margret Anne, 'and the bag is a wreck!'

To console her sister, Mrs Pepperpot brought out one of those plastic dolls, dressed in the latest American fashion and with a pair of jewelled spectacles on just like Margret Anne. How they both laughed! And as they were hungry after all their adventures, they sat down to eat the delicious pancakes and layer-cake.

'I haven't tasted anything so good for forty years,' declared Margret Anne. Then she looked at Mrs Pepperpot and said: 'It's funny, sister, but I always thought of you as such a small person.'

Mrs Pepperpot grinned: 'There are times when I feel pretty small myself!'

Gapy Gob gets a Letter from the King

IT's time we had a story about ogres. D'you remember we met some before?

There was a he-ogre who was called Gapy Gob, because he was so fond of eating he always had his mouth open for more. Then there was a she-ogre, or ogress, whose name was Wily Winnie, because she was always up to some trick or other.

Gapy Gob had two of the nicest little servants: a girl who did the cooking and was called Katie Cook and a boy who chopped the wood, so he was called Charlie Chop. *They* weren't ogres at all, just ordinary children, but they had no home of their own, so they lived with Gapy Gob, and he was very, very fond of them. Wily Winnie also had a servant, a very cunning cat called Ribby Ratsoup.

Gapy Gob and the children lived on the sunny side of a small mountain in a cosy little house with a cow-shed. They had one brown cow, but she only spent the winter in the shed, all spring and summer she grazed on the

high mountain pasture and gave them wonderful milk. While Charlie Chop kept the yard stocked with dry logs to burn on the stove, Katie Cook looked after the garden and saw that they always had plenty of potatoes and other vegetables. If it hadn't been for one thing, they would all three have been as happy and contented as kings.

But on the dark side of the mountain, where the sun never shone, lived Wily Winnie in her dark, untidy mess of a house. Her cat, Ribby Ratsoup, was so lazy that she never swept the floor or made their beds, but if she saw her chance to steal a nice bit of meat or fish, she made a huge steaming bowl of stew (don't ask me what *else* she put in it) and they lived on it for days.

Now these two envied Gapy Gob his nice house and especially his well-stocked larder. For Katie was such a good cook and housewife that she always had a large ham hanging up in the larder and a great bowl of milk with thick cream on top standing on the shelf.

Wily Winnie would have given the last remaining tooth in her big ugly mouth to have a taste of that lovely ham, and Ribby Ratsoup's whiskers trembled when she thought of dipping into that layer of golden cream! But it was no use, Katie always locked the door of the larder very carefully and hung the key on a belt round her waist.

So the ogress and her cat sat in their dark little kitchen and schemed and schemed till one morning in May Ribby came up with an idea.

A little while later, when Charlie Chop was standing in Gapy's yard, chopping wood as usual, he heard a rustling in the wheatfield close by.

'Who's treading down our young wheat?' he asked

loudly. He was pretty sure he knew who it was.

Right enough, out of the corn stalked Ribby Ratsoup with her tail in the air.

'It's only little me,' she minced, and tried to slip past Charlie. But he blocked the cat's way with the axe and demanded sternly: 'What d'you want, you good-for-nothing sly-puss?'

'Tut, tut! Such language!' said Ribby, getting up on her hind legs and dusting herself down. 'I have business with your master which doesn't concern you. Is he at home?'

'Maybe he is and maybe he isn't,' said Charlie, 'but he has no business with *you*, so you can just skip off home!'

'What a very rude servant Gapy Gob keeps,' said Ribby with her nose in the air. 'I shall have to tell him about you. Anyway, I have a letter for him from the King.'

'Rubbish,' said Charlie. 'The King wouldn't send a scruffy cat like you with a letter to my master.'

'That's enough!' said Ribby. 'Actually the postman asked me to deliver the letter, as I was coming this way, and now will you please let me pass!'

So Charlie allowed the cat to go inside the house, where she found Katie at the stove, busy stirring a pot of porridge for Gapy Gob's breakfast.

'Good morning and good appetite!' said Ribby, trying to curtsey with her stiff back legs.

'Good appetite is right,' said Gapy Gob, who was sitting at the table, drumming with his wooden spoon. He was very hungry and didn't like to be kept waiting for his meals.

Katie said nothing, but Ribby walked round the table, purring in her cattiest way: 'Don't worry, Gapy Gob,' she said, 'you'll soon have the most scrumptious porridge. We all know what a good cook Katie is. Of course, in our house we do have breakfast rather earlier, my mistress is so very particular!'

'In this house we eat when the food is ready,' said

Katie crossly, 'and it's no later today than it usually is. Anyhow, what d'you want, Ribby? There are no herrings for you to run off with today, if that's what you're after!'

'What an idea!' said Ribby. 'You and Charlie must both have jumped out of bed the wrong side this morning!' Then she turned her back on Katie and gave Gapy Gob one of those smiles that reach from ear to ear.

'I've brought something for you,' she said.

'What is it?' asked Gapy Gob, who loved getting presents.

'The postman asked me to deliver this letter to you personally,' said Ribby, as she pulled a big envelope from her apron pocket. 'It's from the King.'

Gapy Gob's eyes grew as round as saucers. 'From the King?' he stammered. 'What does he want with me?'

'Let me see,' said Katie, trying to snatch the letter from Ribby.

But Ribby showed her claws and hissed: 'Keep your fingers to yourself, Miss Hoity Toity. The King's writing is so fine it can only be read by cat's eyes.'

'Read it to me, Ribby, there's a good cat,' said Gapy coaxingly, 'and you, Katie, just get on with the porridge.'

Ribby Ratsoup opened the envelope and pulled out a sheet of paper. ' "To Mr Gapy Gob from His Majesty the King," ' she began importantly.

' "As it has come to our notice that Mr Gapy Gob has

been eating more ham and cream—as well as more porridge—than is good for him, we hereby decree that he must from now on live on butter toffees exclusively...."'

'Exclu—whatever-it-is, what does that mean?' asked Gapy Gob.

'To anyone who has had schooling like myself,' said Ribby, twirling her whiskers and looking slyly at poor Katie at the stove, 'it is quite simple. It means that you can only eat butter toffees and *nothing* else at all!'

'Mm, I wouldn't mind that!' said Gapy Gob, who was already licking his chops.

'Can I go on?' asked Ribby.

'Oh yes, please do,' said Gapy.

' "Whatever ham and cream is now in Mr Gapy Gob's larder must be handed over to Madam Wily Winnie immediately. Signed H.M. King." '

Quick as a flash Katie took the letter from Ribby's hand. The writing was so small she couldn't read it and as for the signature, it looked more like a cat's cradle!

'It's all nonsense!' she told Gapy. But he wouldn't listen; he was sure the letter came from the King, and, besides, he liked the idea of eating butter toffees for a change.

'Did the King send any toffees for me?' he asked.

'No,' said Ribby, 'but, as it happens, I have some in my

apron pocket. Here you are!' And she poured a whole pile of toffees in coloured paper wrappings on to the table. 'I'll have to go home to my mistress now, but we'll be back this afternoon for the ham and the cream!'

'Mind you bring some more toffees!' said Gapy Gob, who was already munching three, 'I won't get far with this little handful!'

Ribby promised to bring lots more toffees, and bounded off into the wheatfield, ploughing a great path through the corn, while Charlie Chop tried to hit her with a log of wood.

Inside the house Katie was standing in front of Gapy Gob, her hands on her hips: she was very angry. 'Fancy you believing all that stuff!' she said.

But Gapy Gob was munching his eighth toffee and finding it very, very good. 'The King knows what's best for me,' he said, with his mouth full, 'and nothing you can say will make any difference. You can throw all that porridge out of the window—or eat it yourself, if you like. Just give me my plate and I'll eat the rest of the toffees with a spoon.'

Just then Charlie came in for his breakfast.

'What's Gapy Gob eating?' he asked his sister.

'Butter toffees that Ribby gave him,' she said, 'and he's not even bothering to take off the paper.'

'But you know toffee is bad for his teeth!' said Charlie. 'Anyway, what's wrong with porridge?'

'The King has forbidden me to eat porridge—or ham—or cream; I'm just to eat toffees and it's wonderful!' said Gapy Gob, grinning at them both between munches.

Well, the children gave up after that. They just ladled out some porridge into their own little wooden bowls and ate it up without another word.

By now Gapy Gob had eaten twenty-eight butter toffees and was just starting on his twenty-ninth when suddenly he threw down his spoon and gave a loud wail. 'Ouch!' he shouted, 'it hurts!'

Katie and Charlie took no notice, but just went on eating.

'Ouch!' he shouted again, holding his face in his

hands: 'Can't you see I'm in pain, children? Do something about it!'

'What can *we* do?' asked Katie. 'You'd better write a letter to the King.'

'Or send for Wily Winnie and that clever cat of hers!' said Charlie.

'Don't be like that!' said Gapy Gob, and he put his head on his arms on the table and started to cry. 'I tell you it hurts like anything!' he sobbed.

'Oh, very well,' said Katie to Charlie, 'I suppose we'll have to help him. You bring that scrubbing brush and we'll take him down to the waterfall.'

'What are you going to do with me?' asked poor Gapy Gob.

'Come along now, and don't ask questions,' said Katie, helping him to his feet and leading him outside. Then they took him down to a place where there was a little waterfall over some rocks.

'Now,' said Katie, 'you sit down and lean your head back under the waterfall. That's right!' she said, as Gapy Gob obediently held his head under the rushing water.

'Now open your mouth!' said Katie, and she beckoned to Charlie to start brushing Gapy's teeth. The scrubbing brush was just right, as Gapy's mouth was almost the size of a hippopotamus's.

Poor Gapy Gob! He was nearly choking with the water

pouring into his mouth, and the scrubbing brush tasted of soap and disinfectant, but very soon it was over, and all the sweet, sticky toffee had been washed away.

Katie had brought a towel to dry him with. While he was sitting on the rock she could reach his head, and she rubbed and rubbed till he was quite dry. But Gapy Gob was still unhappy. 'It hasn't stopped hurting! Look, in there, that tooth!' and he pointed inside his mouth.

Charlie climbed on the ogre's knee and peeped in; sure enough, one tooth had a big hole in it!

'No wonder it hurts!' he said. 'I'll soon fix that!' And he went over to a tree-stump and pulled off a big lump of resin (that's the gummy stuff that oozes out of trees). He rolled in into a nice ball in his fingers—just like the dentist does—and plugged it into Gapy's tooth.

'That's better,' said Gapy Gob, 'it's stopped hurting altogether!' Then they all went back to the house and the ogre thanked both his faithful servants.

'I never want to see another butter toffee in all my life,' he declared, 'and I don't care *what* the King says!'

'It's not the King you have to worry about,' said Katie. 'What about Wily Winnie and Ribby Ratsoup who are coming here this afternoon to fetch the ham and the bowl of cream?'

'Oh dear, oh dear, I'd forgotten about that!' wailed Gapy Gob. 'What shall I do?'

'Don't worry,' said Charlie, 'we'll find a way to fix those two minxes.'

So, in the afternoon, when the ogress and her servant, the cat, arrived, they were ready for them.

Wily Winnie and Ribby Ratsoup were a bit nervous. 'You knock!' said Wily to the cat.

'No, you do it!' said Ribby, and then the door opened

and they both fell into the kitchen in a heap.

'Hullo!' said Gapy Gob, and gave them both a pleasant smile.

Wily Winnie picked herself up. 'We've just come for . . .' and then she didn't know what more to say.

But Katie helped her out. 'Oh yes,' she said, 'we've packed up the ham in a paper parcel and put a cloth over the cream bowl, so that it won't upset when you carry it. Here it is, all ready for you on the table. We hope you will enjoy it as much as our master enjoyed the toffees. Did you bring him some more toffees?'

'Oh, no!' cried Gapy Gob. backing into a corner. 'No more toffees—ever!'

'Well . . . Thank you very much!' said the ogress. 'We'll be off home then. Come on, Ribby, you carry the cream.' And she took the large paper parcel from the table and walked out, followed by Ribby, carefully balancing the covered bowl between her paws.

As soon as they were out of sight of the house, Wily turned to Ribby. 'Let me have a taste of your cream,' she said, and put out her hand for the bowl.

'Oh no,' said Ribby, holding on to the bowl, 'not till you give me a slice of your ham!'

In the tussle that followed, the bowl fell on the ground and the contents started running down the road.

'Look what you've done!' shouted Ribby.

'How dare you answer me back!' shouted Wily Winnie, and she hit the cat over the head with the paper parcel. It gave a great crack, and out flew—not a ham, but an old broom with a broken handle!

'Of all the dirty tricks!' said the ogress, and stamped her foot so hard it made the ground tremble.

But Ribby was down on all fours, trying to save some of the cream by licking it up. She took one taste and then she spat it out, right into Wily Winnie's face!

'It's white paint!' she hissed. 'We've been double-crossed!'

Much later, when Gapy Gob and the children went for their evening walk to watch the sun go down, they could see Wily Winnie many miles away, running up and down the mountain, still chasing her cat with that old broom! And they laughed and they laughed and they laughed!

Mrs Pepperpot and the Budgerigar

NEAR Mrs Pepperpot's house stands a very pretty little cottage with a garden round it. There is also a handsome double gate decorated with trees and flowers and leaves, all made of wrought iron and painted shiny black. Entwined in the leaves on one side of the gate is the word 'Happy' and on the other the word 'Home'. So when the gate is shut it reads 'Happy Home'. As a matter of fact, the cottage belongs to a Mr and Mrs Happy. The wife's first name is Bella, but no one's ever heard the husband's first name, as he hardly ever speaks to anyone, but just sits under the sunshade in the garden and reads his newspaper. Mrs Pepperpot thinks 'Mr Glum' would have suited him better.

The Happys are only there in the summer holidays, but then Mrs Pepperpot sees quite a lot of Mrs Happy. She pops over to borrow a bit of rhubarb or a cup of flour, or to snip a few chives or some parsley. This goes on nearly every day, and they always have a little chat and then Mrs Happy says: 'You really must come and visit

me one of these days and meet my Pipkins—he is such a darling bird!'

Pipkins is Mrs Happy's budgerigar, which she brings with her from town, so that he too can have a nice country holiday.

'He's getting so clever at talking,' said Mrs Happy one day. 'I've taught him to say four whole words now. As soon as I have a free day, Mrs Pepperpot, I'll invite you over.'

Mrs Pepperpot had never seen a budgerigar and was very curious to hear a bird talking, so she thanked Mrs Happy and hoped she'd soon be asked.

But the days went by, and although Mrs Happy still kept coming over for this and that which she'd forgotten to buy at the store, she always seemed to be too busy to invite Mrs Pepperpot to her house.

Then one morning Mrs Pepperpot had been picking sugar-peas for her husband's supper and she found she had quite a lot over.

'I could take them over to Mrs Happy,' she said to herself. 'Then perhaps she would let me have a look at that budgery—thing-e-me-jig. I'd dearly like to hear a bird talk.'

So she put on her best apron and scarf, popped the peas in a paper bag and walked over to 'Happy Home'. She went through the wrought-iron gate, up the path and through the open front door. Inside the hall she knocked on one of the closed doors. No one answered, but she

could hear Mrs Happy talking to someone inside.

'Come on, darling,' she was saying, 'just to please me, say "Thank you, Mama!" '

'That's funny,' thought Mrs Pepperpot, 'I never knew Mrs Happy had any children.' She knocked again.

'Wait a minute, my love,' said Mrs Happy inside, 'there's someone at the door.' And she opened the door just a tiny crack.

'Oh, it's you, Mrs Pepperpot,' she said, slipping through the door and shutting it behind her. 'How kind of you to call.'

'I just brought you these peas from the garden,' said Mrs Pepperpot and handed her the bag.

'Thank you so much; I love sugar-peas!' said Mrs Happy. 'I wish I could ask you in, but just now I'm busy with my little boy . . .'

'You never told me you had a son,' said Mrs Pepperpot.

Mrs Happy laughed. 'Oh dear, no, I mean my Pipkins, my little budgie! He's all I have, you know, and just now I'm making him practise the words he can say, so that my friends can hear him when they come to tea this afternoon. They're coming all the way from town.'

'Well, I'll be going then,' said Mrs Pepperpot, who was a bit disappointed at not being asked in.

'Come round tomorrow morning,' said Mrs Happy, 'and have a cup of coffee and help me finish up the cakes.'

When she got home Mrs Pepperpot remembered that she hadn't time next morning, as that was her washing day.

'I'll slip over later and tell her I can't come,' she said to herself. So, about three o'clock, she walked over to the cottage and again she found the front door open, so she went into the hall and knocked on one of the inner doors. As there was no reply, she opened the door and found herself in the sitting-room. It was all ready for the tea-party, she could see, with a pretty white cloth on the table, the best china set out and a big vase of flowers. On a smaller table by the window stood a cage.

Mrs Pepperpot couldn't resist going over to have a look at the pretty blue bird which was swinging to and fro on its perch. She sat down on the table beside the cage and said: 'Hullo, Pipkins, are you going to talk to me?'

The bird just looked at her.

'I don't believe it *can* talk!' said Mrs Pepperpot, and as she said that she felt herself SHRINK!

'So you don't believe I can talk,' said the budgerigar, but now, of course, he was talking bird-language, which Mrs Pepperpot could understand when she grew small.

'Well,' said Mrs Pepperpot, 'I hadn't *heard* you talking till now.' She was standing on the table, wondering how she was going to get away before Mrs Happy and her guests came in.

'As a matter of fact,' said the bird, 'you've come just at the right moment. I want you to help me.'

'Help *you*? How can I help you when I don't even know how to help myself just now?' said Mrs Pepperpot, walking all round the cage to see if there was anything she could climb down by. But she was trapped!

'Well, I want to play a trick on Mrs Happy,' said the bird.

'A trick, Pipkins, what sort of a trick?' asked Mrs Pepperpot.

'Please don't call me by that stupid name. Pipkins, indeed; my real name is "Suchislife". Don't you think that sounds more superior?' The budgerigar was preening his feathers as he spoke, and looking down his beak at Mrs Pepperpot.

'Oh yes,' she said hurriedly, 'very superior!' Secretly she thought it sounded like something her husband usually said when he hadn't won the ski-race: 'Ah well, such is life!'

'What d'you want me to do?' she asked the bird.

'I'll explain,' said Suchislife. 'But we must be quick, as Mrs Happy has only gone down the hill to meet her guests. First, will you open the door of the cage, please?'

Mrs Pepperpot did as she was asked and unhinged the cage door.

'Now, just step inside,' went on the bird, and Mrs Pepperpot walked into the cage.

No sooner was she in than the budgerigar hopped out and, quick as lightning, fastened the door-hinge with his beak!

'Got you!' he chirped merrily and flapped his wings with excitement.

Mrs Pepperpot glared at him through the bars. 'You needn't think you can be funny with me!' she said, 'or I shall take back my offer to help!'

'Sorry, ma'am!' he said. 'When I get my freedom it sort of goes to my head, don't you know. But please don't be angry; just listen to my plan.' He had flown up on top of the cage, and took hold of the cover which was hooked on to it. 'I'm going to put the cover on,' he said, as he pulled it neatly down over the cage with his beak, making it quite dark for Mrs Pepperpot inside.

'Now,' said the bird, 'Mrs Happy won't notice that you're in there instead of me. She'll want me to do my party piece to impress her precious guests, so when you hear her say: "Come on, pet, say 'Thank you, Mama' and 'Pipkins Happy'," you just tell her what you think of her.'

'But you haven't told me why you don't like her,' objected Mrs Pepperpot.

'She's mean, and for all her talk about how clever I am, she neglects me. I often have to go without fresh water or she forgets to give me any grain. But you'll soon see what she's like.' And with that Suchislife flew out of the window and hid in a tree to watch what would happen.

Mrs Pepperpot had just settled herself comfortably on the budgerigar's swing when she heard the ladies come into the sitting-room.

'D'you think it can really talk?' she heard one of them say.

'Four words; think of that!' said the second lady.

'Wonderful, isn't it?' said the third lady.

Mrs Pepperpot didn't know what to do. She could hear Mrs Happy getting the tea ready in the kitchen, and now she heard the ladies coming nearer the cage.

'Shall we have a peep at it?' asked the first lady.

'D'you think we dare?' said the second.

'We could just lift the cover a little bit,' suggested the third.

But at the moment a little voice from inside the cage squeaked: 'Don't touch the cover!'

'How very strange,' said the first lady. 'It said four words exactly. Mrs Happy! Your budgie has just talked to us—we heard it clearly.'

Mrs Happy came in with the cakes; she was so taken up with getting the tea served, that she didn't ask *what* words the bird had said. She didn't even notice the cover was on.

'My Pipkins is so clever! Now do sit down all of you and make yourselves at home.' And they all sat down and started chattering the way ladies do, and Mrs Pepperpot stayed as quiet as if she had really been a budgerigar under the cover. But she listened to every word that was being said.

'I must tell you,' said Mrs Happy, laughing gaily, 'about the funny neighbour I have just down the road. She's a little old woman with long skirts and a shawl, and she wears her hair scraped back like something from Grandma's time. She's a scream! She will come tripping in here, knocking at the door . . .'

From the cage came an indignant squeak: 'You invited her yourself!'

For a moment Mrs Happy didn't know what to say, but then she laughed again: 'Isn't he funny? You'd almost think he was joining in the conversation, but, of course, he doesn't know what he's saying. I'll get him to say his name, but first I'll take the cover off so you can see him.' And she got up to do this.

'Don't touch the cover!' squeaked the voice from the cage.

'That's what it said before!' said one of the ladies.

'How very odd!' said Mrs Happy. 'Perhaps someone else has been teaching him to talk while I was out. Well, we won't bother with him just now. I was telling you about the funny old woman down the road; she has the quaintest little house . . .'

'That's not what you say when you go borrowing rhubarb and sugar and eggs and parsley and anything else you've forgotten to buy. The little old woman's good enough for that, Mrs Snobby Happy!'

All the ladies were aghast. Mrs Happy jumped up and ran to the table to snatch off the cover. But her foot slipped and she fell, knocking the whole cage out of the open window!

While the ladies screamed and picked up Mrs Happy, Suchislife flew down from the tree where he'd been hiding. He quickly unhinged the cage door and let Mrs Pepperpot out. Then he hopped in himself and Mrs Pepperpot shut the door behind him.

'Well done!' he said. 'I watched the whole performance and you certainly gave that old cat just the right medicine.'

Mrs Pepperpot was still shaking with anger. 'She won't be wanting to borrow from me again in a hurry! Of all the ungrateful, two-faced . . .' But Mrs Pepperpot didn't have time to finish her sentence because just then she grew to her normal size. She picked up the cage with Suchislife inside and knocked on the front door.

Inside there was so much noise going on that they

didn't hear Mrs Pepperpot's knock, so she walked in.

What a sight! Mrs Happy was lying on the sofa, moaning and holding her head, while two of her guests were mopping up the third who had had the whole pot of tea spilt over her! They didn't seem to see Mrs Pepperpot, so she put the cage on the table and said: 'I found this in the garden. I suppose it must be the bird you were telling me about, the one that talks so well?'

'Take it away, Mrs Pepperpot, take it away!' groaned Mrs Happy. 'I never want to see it again!'

'But I thought it was the cleverest bird alive,' said Mrs Pepperpot, who could hardly keep from smiling.

'It's far too clever for me,' said Mrs Happy, 'and I'd be pleased if you would accept it as a present—in return for all the nice things you've done for me this summer.'

'Don't mention it, Mrs Happy,' said Mrs Pepperpot,

'but I'd be glad to take Suchis life—I mean Pipkins—home, if you really don't want him any more.'

Then Mrs Pepperpot carried the cage out of the door, down the path and through the handsome wrought-iron gates, and the little blue bird just jumped and down inside, saying one word over and over again: 'Happy, happy, happy, happy!'

'I'm happy too,' said Mrs Pepperpot.